Murder on the Ferry
The Prequel to the Jessie Harper Paranormal Mysteries
KJ Cornwall

Hendry Publishing

Copyright © 2024 by KJ Cornwall

All rights reserved.

No portion of this book may be reproduced in any form without written permission from the publisher or author, except as permitted by U.S. copyright law.

This book is a work of fiction. Names, characters, business, organisations, places and events other than those clearly in the public domain, are either the product of the author's imagination or are used fictitiously.

Second Ed.

Contents

1. Prologue — 1
2. Liverpool, England 1930s — 5
3. Elsie — 18
4. The Royal Iris II Mersey Ferry — 30
5. The Council — 35
6. Help — 47
7. More Help — 62
8. The Other Crime Scenes — 77
9. Margaret — 88
10. A Discovery — 104
11. Betrayal — 110
12. Hostage — 123
13. Otherworldly Power — 136
14. Who Did I Kill? — 145
15. Doubts — 157

16.	Revealed	168
17.	Fire and Adversity	182
18.	A Dream	189
19.	Epilogue	201
Acknowledgements		212
About the Author		213
Also By		216

Prologue

1917 YPRES, BELGIUM

THE DAMP CHILL OF the trenches clung to Corporal George Jenkin's uniform as he trudged through the muck and mud. The constant thud of artillery reverberated through the air, making conversation nearly impossible. Yet, in those moments of respite between barrages, George and Lieutenant Bill Roberts found solace in each other's company.

The 4th (Extra Reserve) Battalion of the King's (Liverpool Regiment) had become their shared reality. Life and death danced on the razor's edge and camaraderie forged in the crucible of war was unbreakable. George, a young recruit with dreams of becoming a policeman, and Bill, the same age as George but already a seasoned soldier and commissioned officer in the British Army possessed a stoic demeanour. They shared a bond that surpassed the horrors of the battlefield.

It was during the relentless onslaught in Ypres that their connection solidified. Shells exploded overhead, raining shrapnel and chaos upon the trench. George, caught in the crossfire, felt a searing pain in his leg as a piece of shrapnel tore through the flesh of his right leg. He crumpled to the ground, blood staining the mud.

Bill, with a calmness that belied the chaos around them, rushed to George's side. The stench of death and decay hung heavy in the air as Bill assessed the wound. Applying makeshift bandages and providing words of reassurance, Bill worked diligently to stabilise his comrade.

The barrage intensified, and evacuation became imperative. With unwavering bravery, Bill hoisted George onto his shoulder, navigating the treacherous trench with the weight of his injured friend. Through the mud, the darkness, and the deafening explosions, Bill carried George to safety.

For his actions that day, Bill Roberts earned the Military Medal—an accolade for gallantry and devotion to duty under the relentless fire of battle. It was a symbol of the unspoken heroism that defined their wartime experience. Yet, despite the recognition, Bill remained reticent about the events at Ypres. He never spoke of the terror, the pain, or the selflessness that earned him that medal.

The two-column article in the Liverpool Daily Post was also a symbol of Bill's heroism and was avidly read by an auburn-haired schoolgirl by the name of Jessie Harper.

She didn't know Bill but she knew George as the son of family friends and they spent a lot of their school holidays together despite George being her senior by a few years. Jessie had always thought of George as the big brother she never had.

1930s

Back in the present, the memory of that fateful day lingered between George and Bill like a silent oath. George, haunted by the spectres of war, found solace in the fact that Bill was the only one privy to his dreams of becoming a policeman in his native Liverpool. The weight of their shared history allowed Bill to understand George's unspoken aspirations that had turned into frustration.

In 1920, Bill Roberts, the soldier became Police Constable Bill Roberts of the Liverpool City Police having turned his back on the family farm in North Wales. In the same year, George was unsuccessful in his application to join the Liverpool City Police. He was turned down owing to his war wound that necessitated him using a cane as an aid to help him walk.

In 1925 Bill Roberts was promoted to Sergeant and transferred to the CID at Liverpool's Hatton Garden police station. Detective Sergeant Roberts wasted no time in helping George secure a job as a CID Admin assistant at Hatton Garden.

Now, in a dimly lit room, the two veterans sat, surrounded by the echoes of a war that refused to be forgotten. The clink of glasses and the muted sounds of a bustling pub formed a backdrop for their conversation. With a rare glint of vulnerability in his eyes, George confided in Bill about his plans for the future.

"I want to make a difference, Bill. To bring justice where it's needed," George admitted his words carrying the weight of the unspoken pact formed on the battlefield. "If I can do that as a CID clerk, so be it."

Bill, though a man of few words, nodded in understanding. The bond forged in the crucible of war had transcended time, allowing Bill to comprehend George's unspoken desires. With a shared history etched in the scars of Ypres, George's hopes for the future were not just George's dream but a testament to the enduring brotherhood born in the fires of World War I.

Liverpool, England 1930s

Jessie Harper stood by the window of her modest rented flat in the Sefton Park district of Liverpool, her auburn hair framing her delicate face as she peered out into the bustling streets. Her hazel eyes, wide with curiosity and a hint of mischievous sparkle, scanned the passers-by, always on the lookout for anything unusual or otherworldly. At thirty-three, Jessie exuded an air of elegance and sophistication, which was only enhanced by her 1930s-inspired wardrobe that clung to her tall, slender frame.

Her fascination with the paranormal had begun at a young age, fuelled by stories of ghostly encounters and unexplained phenomena whispered in hushed tones among the residents of her beloved city. She had spent countless hours poring over dusty tomes and rare manuscripts, seeking to unravel the mysteries hidden within their ancient pages. This fascination in turn led her to specialising in the paranormal at the library where she worked.

"Meow."

Jessie glanced down at the source of the noise: Khan, her loyal feline companion. This sleek black cat with striking green eyes had been a fixture in her life for years. No one knew where he had come from. He simply materialised one day alongside Jessie in the library where she worked. It seemed like he had been drawn to her side by some unseen force.

Jessie had given the cat an unusual name, for a cat, of Khan. Jessie knew the origin of the cat's name. He was named after a hero in the Great War of 1914 - 1918, Khudadad Khan: the first Muslim soldier to receive the Victoria Cross when his small team of machine gunners stalled a German advance long enough to allow for British reinforcements to arrive in October 1914.

"Hello, Khan," Jessie murmured, stroking his silky fur affectionately. "What do you make of the world today?"

Khan replied, "Curiouser and curiouser, Jessie," his voice was smooth and distinctly human. Jessie was the only human who knew Khan could talk. "I heard your landlord telling someone I was your familiar."

"I knew it." Jessie said, "Now, Khan, it's more important than ever that no one suspects you can talk or that I can hear you. Some bigots may say I'm a witch and we can't be having that now, can we? No, don't answer."

Jessie reclined on her plush sofa, a soft cashmere throw draped over her legs. The warm glow of the firelight cast dancing shadows across the room, illuminating the shelves that lined the walls, bending under the weight of books dedicated to the paranormal. The scent of old leather and musty parchment intermingled with the sweet aroma of her chamomile tea. She savoured each sip, allowing the soothing liquid to wash away the fatigue of the day.

"Khan, can you imagine how thrilling it would be to actually experience one of these supernatural encounters?" Jessie mused aloud, her voice barely more than a whisper as she stared into the flickering flames.

"Sometimes I wonder if there's more to this world than meets the eye," she continued, her gaze shifting to the worn spine of a book titled 'Ghosts of Liverpool's Past.' "But who am I to assume such extraordinary things could happen to someone like me?"

"Meow," Khan replied nonchalantly, his green eyes fixed on the fire. He languidly stretched, his black tail flicking in contentment.

"Quite right, Khan," Jessie chuckled, gently stroking his fur. "Life is full of surprises."

"Indeed, it is Jessie," Khan said, his voice now deep and resonant. "Jessie," Khan said softly, "I understand how unusual this must appear. Allow me to explain once more."

He shifted his position on the couch as he continued. "You see, I have been granted the ability to communicate with you because you possess a rare and special gift. You are attuned to the supernatural world."

Jessie's mouth hung open but she couldn't deny the curiosity that bubbled within her. A dozen questions formed in her mind, each vying for attention.

"Supernatural world?" Jessie repeated, her voice barely audible. Her heart raced and she instinctively reached for her teacup, seeking solace in the familiar warmth. "I've always been fascinated by the paranormal, but to be involved in it myself... Are you saying that I can actually interact with spirits or something of that sort?"

"Something like that," Khan replied, his green eyes never leaving hers. "Your connection to the supernatural is strong, and with my help, we can explore and develop your abilities further."

Jessie sat back against the cushions, her mind reeling. It was as if the characters from her favourite books had suddenly come to life, inviting her into their mysterious realm. She felt a strange mix of fear and exhilaration course through her veins.

"Khan, you need to understand that this is quite a lot to take in," Jessie finally forced herself to say. "How am I to believe that any of this is real?"

"Trust in yourself and in our bond, Jessie," Khan urged, his gaze unwavering. "Together, we can unlock the secrets of the supernatural world around us."

Jessie hesitated, her thoughts swirling like a whirlwind. Was she truly prepared to delve into this unknown territory? She glanced around the room, at the stacks of books that had provided solace and entertainment for so many years. Could she turn her back on the opportunity to experience what she'd only read about?

"Alright," Jessie said, her voice filled with a sense of purpose as she looked back at Khan. "If you believe in me, then I'm willing to give it a try." Inside, her heart threatened to burst with anticipation, but she maintained a calm exterior. "What comes next?"

"First, we must learn more about your gift, and then we can embark on our journey together," Khan replied, satisfaction flickering in his eyes. "I promise, Jessie, the world you are about to enter is more wondrous than you could ever imagine."

As Jessie stared at her talking cat, the curiosity that had always driven her fascination with the paranormal ignited anew. With a deep breath, she steeled herself for the adventures and mysteries that awaited her and Khan.

"Are you ready?" Khan asked, his whiskers quivering with anticipation.

Jessie nodded, her heart racing. "As ready as I'll ever be."

"Very well," Khan said, his green eyes focused on a spot in the room. His tail twitched, and then he began to speak in a low, melodic chant. Jessie watched in awe as the air around them seemed to shimmer like heat rising from a sun-baked road.

Before long, a ghostly figure began to materialise beside the fireplace. It was an older woman, garbed in a flowing Victorian-era dress, her hair piled high upon her head. The apparition turned to look at Jessie and Khan, a bemused expression crossing her translucent face.

"Mrs Cruickshank!" Jessie gasped, recognising the spirit of a former teacher. She had read about her tragic demise in one of her paranormal books but never dreamed she would actually encounter her ghost.

"Hello, dear," Mrs Cruickshank said, her voice ethereal yet soothing. "I see you've made the acquaintance of Mr Khan."

"Indeed," Khan replied, dipping his head in respect. "We are here to learn more about Jessie's gift and how best to use it."

"Ah, yes." Mrs Cruickshank floated closer, examining Jessie with a keen eye. "You have great potential, my dear. With proper guidance and practice, you'll be able to interact with all manner of spirits, not just those already bound to this plane."

Jessie's mind raced with excitement, her earlier doubts fading as she considered the possibilities. Communicating with the dead, solving ancient mysteries, perhaps even encountering famous historical figures—her life was about to become far more thrilling than she'd ever dared to imagine.

"Thank you, Mrs Cruickshank," Jessie breathed, her eyes gleaming with enthusiasm. "I promise I'll do my best not to squander this opportunity."

"Very well," the ghostly woman said, giving Jessie an approving nod. "Now, let us begin your training."

As Jessie and Khan settled onto the soft rug before the fireplace, Mrs Cruickshank outlined the fundamentals of spirit communication. Jessie listened attentively, her mind awhirl with newfound knowledge and burgeoning power.

"Remember, dear," Mrs Cruickshank reminded her as their lesson drew to a close, "to always treat the spirits you encounter with respect and empathy. Many are lost or confused, and it falls to you to help guide them."

"I understand," Jessie replied solemnly, feeling the weight of her responsibility settle upon her shoulders. "And I'm grateful for your guidance."

"Of course, child," Mrs Cruickshank said, her spectral form beginning to fade. "Now go forth and embrace your destiny."

"Goodbye, Mrs Cruickshank," Jessie murmured as the ghost vanished completely, leaving her alone with Khan in her room.

"Are you ready to embark on this journey, Jessie?" Khan asked, his green eyes sparkling with excitement.

"More than ever," she replied, her voice full of anticipation. Together, they would explore the shadowy realms that had long captivated her imagination, forging a bond that would transcend life and death itself.

A Few Days Later

As Jessie Harper stood in front of her cheval mirror, she couldn't help but admire the way her auburn shoulder-length hair framed her heart-shaped face. She had just finished pinning it up into a stylish bob, which was all the rage in 1930s Liverpool. Her eyes sparkled with excitement as they took in the elegant attire she had selected for the evening: a deep green velvet frock adorned with intricate beadwork, and a matching cloche hat that hugged the curve of her head.

"Looking good, Jessie," Khan remarked, his voice calm and soothing. "You'll surely stand out in the crowd."

"Thank you, Khan." Jessie smiled at her feline companion, grateful for his presence and unwavering support. "We have an important event to attend tonight, after all."

"Indeed," Khan replied, his green eyes fixed on hers. "Your first real experience with the supernatural world awaits."

Jessie's whole being was filled with anticipation as she stepped back from the mirror and walked toward the window. Gazing out onto the bustling streets of Liverpool, she marvelled at the lively atmosphere that embraced the city. The air was thick with the scent of chimney smoke, mingling with the aroma of fresh-baked goods wafting from the corner bakery. Men in dapper three-piece suits wearing the latest fashion in hats hurried by alongside women attired in smart dresses, wearing cloche hats. Their laughter and chatter create a symphony of life.

"Sometimes I can hardly believe this is real," Jessie mused aloud, her thoughts drifting to the ghostly encounter she had shared with Khan just a few days prior. "But it's all happening, isn't it?"

"Indeed, it is," Khan confirmed, leaping gracefully onto the windowsill beside her. "And it's only the beginning,

Jessie. Together, we'll uncover mysteries and secrets long hidden from human sight."

Jessie nodded, feeling a mixture of excitement and trepidation wash over her. She took one last look at the bustling cityscape in the near distance - the iconic Liver Building standing tall against the skyline, its mythical liver birds perched atop, watching over the city with a protective gaze.

"Alright," she said as she turned to Khan. "Let's get going."

"Lead the way, Jessie." Khan encouraged, his tail flicking playfully behind him.

As they made their way along the cobblestone streets, Jessie couldn't help but feel a sense of pride swell within her. This was her city, rich with history and folklore that had long captivated her imagination. And now, with Khan by her side, she would delve deeper into its mysteries than ever before.

"Here's to new adventures, Khan," Jessie whispered, her eyes alive with anticipation.

"Indeed, Jessie," Khan replied softly, his eyes shimmering in the lamplight. "To new adventures."

As they strolled down the bustling streets of Liverpool, the lively chatter of vendors and passers-by filled the air. The rich aroma of fish and chips wafted from nearby street carts as Jessie admired the intricate architecture of the buildings lining the waterfront. Her fashionable 1930s attire drew admiring glances from those she passed.

"Khan, do you know that this city was built on folklore and legends?" Jessie asked, her eyes sparkling with passion.

"Is that so?" the cat replied, genuinely intrigued. "Tell me more."

"Well," Jessie began, her voice filled with enthusiasm, "in the heart of the city lies St James Cemetery, where it's said that restless spirits wander at night. And don't even get me started on the tales of the Williamson Tunnels – a labyrinth of underground passages rumoured to be haunted by the ghost of its builder."

"Ah, I see why you're so fascinated by the paranormal, Jessie," Khan purred. "Your city is steeped in mystery."

Jessie grinned, her love for Liverpool shining in her eyes. "It truly is. And now, with your help, we may finally uncover some of these chilling secrets."

"Indeed," Khan agreed.

"Alright, then," Jessie said, taking a deep breath to calm the excitement coursing through her veins. "Our first stop is the old, abandoned manor on the outskirts of town. There are whispers of strange happenings there, and I've always wanted to investigate."

"Sounds thrilling," Khan mused, his curiosity piqued. "I'm eager to put my abilities to good use."

"Then let's not waste any more time," Jessie declared, her resolve unwavering.

As they made their way towards the manor, Jessie's mind raced with possibilities. What secrets lay hidden within its walls? Who – or what – could be responsible for the strange occurrences reported by those brave enough to venture inside?

"Jessie," Khan said, pulling her from her thoughts. "I can sense your excitement but remember to stay focused. We must approach this investigation with caution."

"Of course, Khan," Jessie agreed, nodding her head resolutely. "We'll uncover the truth together."

As the sun dipped below the horizon, painting the sky a fiery orange, Jessie and Khan arrived at the abandoned manor. The imposing structure loomed over them, casting ominous shadows on the ground beneath their feet.

"Ready, Khan?" Jessie asked, her voice steady but laced with anticipation.

"Always, Jessie," the cat replied, his eyes glowing in the fading light.

With that, they stepped forward into the unknown, their first paranormal investigation unfolding before them. Together, they would delve into the heart of Liverpool's mysteries and embrace the thrilling adventures that awaited them in the world beyond. And as they crossed the threshold into the darkness, their story was only just beginning.

Elsie

REFRESHED AND INVIGORATED BY the introduction to the supernatural world, Jessie thanked Khan for showing her things she had never seen or heard before during the visit to the abandoned manor. A few days after that trip, the police at New Brighton contacted her with some shocking news. Her dear friend, Elsie, had been pushed overboard into the River Mersey from a Mersey ferry. Elsie had drowned and the police asked that Jessie identify the body as they could not contact her husband.

AS JESSIE BOARDED THE Mersey ferry at Liverpool's Landing Stage, she was enveloped by the pulsing energy of 1930s Liverpool. The lively chatter of passengers, the piercing cries of seagulls overhead, and the thrumming beat of the boat's engine combined into an intoxicating symphony. Standing at the railing, she was entranced as a breathtaking landscape unfolded before her - the river's shimmering surface reflecting the sun's golden rays, while the city's imposing skyline loomed in the distance, a symbol of its industrial dominance.

"Another glorious day on the Mersey, isn't it?" remarked a fellow passenger, a rugged man with a grizzled beard and weathered features.

"Absolutely," Jessie replied, her mind momentarily pulled back from dwelling on the sad fate of her friend, Elsie. "This view never fails to take my breath away."

"I've been taking this trip for years," the man chuckled. "And yet every time feels like the first."

Jessie smiled politely before turning her gaze back to the water. She felt a familiar flutter in her stomach, a sign of her deep-rooted connection to the paranormal. As she peered into the depths of the river, she couldn't help but wonder about the enigmas lying hidden beneath its surface – much like those lurking within her own heart.

Jessie's thoughts turned once more to her friend, Elsie. They had been inseparable since their first encounter at the local spiritualist meeting five years ago. Their shared passion for the paranormal had forged a bond that transcended mere friendship, making them more like sisters. They had spent countless evenings discussing everything from ghostly apparitions to mysterious psychic phenomena, always eager to delve deeper into the unseen world around them. As she stared into the depths of the river, she couldn't help but ponder the mysteries that lay hidden beneath the surface – much like those that existed within her own heart.

The ferry continued its journey across the river, each churning wave serving as a reminder of the relentless passage of time. And as Jessie took in the sights and sounds around her, she couldn't help but feel a sense of longing - a desire to uncover the truth behind Elsie's untimely demise, and an unshakable conviction that her own unique gifts would play a crucial role in solving the case.

"Are you alright, miss?" the bearded man asked, concern etched on his face as he noticed Jessie's pensive expression.

"Ah, yes," Jessie replied, shaking off her thoughts. "Just lost in thought, I suppose."

"Understandable," the man said with a knowing nod. "Well, if you ever need someone to talk to, don't hesitate to strike up a conversation. The ferry can be a lonely place sometimes."

"Thank you," Jessie said, touched by the stranger's kindness. "I'll keep that in mind."

As the ferry approached its destination at New Brighton on the opposite riverbank, Jessie's determination to seek justice for Elsie only grew stronger. She knew that the journey ahead would be full of danger and uncertainty, but she also knew that she couldn't turn back now. With each passing moment, the bond she shared with Elsie - and the world of the supernatural - seemed to pull her deeper into the mystery surrounding her friend's murder.

As the ferry docked and Jessie disembarked, she couldn't help but feel that she was taking her first steps towards unravelling the truth - not just about Elsie, but about herself as well.

Jessie's heart contracted, the weight of the news settling in; Elsie was gone. The realisation struck her like a bolt of lightning, sending shivers down her spine. Tears welled up in her eyes as she tried to grasp the enormity of her loss. Her dear friend, the one who had shared countless nights discussing paranormal mysteries and unexplained phenomena, was now intertwined in a mystery of her own.

"Ah, Miss Jessie," a soft, velvety voice cooed, pulling her from the depths of her despair. Khan had appeared at her feet. His fur, though short and as dark as the night sky, seemed to ripple with each graceful stride.

"How on earth..." Jessie stopped, realising he had magical skills. He could make himself invisible as well as talk to Jessie.

"Khan," she whispered, her voice choked by her grief. "Elsie... she's been murdered."

"Murdered?" Khan's eyes widened with sympathy and concern. He brushed against Jessie's leg, his silky fur providing a small comfort in this moment of profound sorrow. "I am so sorry, Miss Jessie. I know how much she meant to you."

Jessie wiped away her tears, feeling the warmth of Khan's presence. It was no secret that their connection was unique; after all, it wasn't every day that one could communicate with a talking cat. But in times like these, Jessie couldn't be more grateful for the solace and support that Khan provided.

"Thank you, Khan," Jessie said, her voice still trembling. "I can't believe she's gone. We were supposed to go on another adventure together, explore more hidden realms of the supernatural world."

"Loss is never easy, Miss Jessie," Khan replied gently, his tail flicking thoughtfully. "But we must remember those we've lost and carry on in their memory."

Jessie took a deep breath, the pain in her chest slowly easing. Khan was right; she couldn't let Elsie's death be in vain. If anything, it made her more resolute in her desire to understand the paranormal world and uncover the truth behind her friend's murder.

"Khan," Jessie said determinedly, "will you help me? I need to find out what happened to Elsie, and I know that your knowledge of the supernatural may be key to unlocking this mystery."

"Of course, Miss Jessie," Khan purred, "I will stand by your side, as I always have. Together, we will seek justice for Elsie and uncover the dark secrets hidden within the shadows."

Jessie and Khan prepared for the investigation that lay ahead. And as they delved deeper into the enigmatic world of the paranormal, their bond would only grow stronger, fuelled by their shared desire for truth and justice.

"Miss Jessie," Khan said softly, his whiskers twitching in the breeze, "I can sense your determination to find out the truth about Elsie's death. I know this is not just another mystery for you."

Jessie turned to face the talking cat, her eyes shimmering with unshed tears. "You're right, Khan. Elsie was like a sister to me. We shared so much together, especially our passion for the paranormal. I can't let her death go unsolved; it feels like there's an invisible thread connecting me to this case."

"Then we shall follow that thread together, Miss Jessie," Khan replied, his green eyes locking onto hers with unwavering loyalty.

As the ferry chugged along, Jessie made her decision. She would take matters into her own hands, embracing her independent nature to investigate Elsie's murder knowing that she couldn't trust anyone else with this task. It was up to her to seek the truth and bring justice to her friend.

"Khan," Jessie murmured, her gaze returning to the river, "I'm going to do this. I don't care how dangerous it may be. I need to find out what happened to Elsie, and I won't rest until I've uncovered every last secret."

"Very well, Miss Jessie," Khan said, his tail flicking in approval. "But remember, you are not alone. I will be with you every step of the way, guiding you through the shadows of the supernatural world."

"Thank you, Khan," Jessie whispered, her hand reaching down to stroke his soft fur. "Together, we will solve this mystery and honour Elsie's memory."

"Indeed, Miss Jessie," Khan purred.

"Promise me you'll guide me through this, Khan," Jessie whispered, her voice wavering. "I don't know if I can do it alone."

"You will never be alone with me by your side. You may not always be able to see me but I'm there... always," Khan said.

Jessie bit her lip, her mind racing as she processed Khan's words. She knew he was right; she had come too far to let fear hold her back. But still, the thought of navigating the shadowy world of the paranormal frightened her. The unknown was vast, and she felt as though she were stepping off the edge of a cliff into darkness.

Jessie took a deep breath, inhaling the salty air as she sought to steady her racing heart. It was true that she had never faced a test quite like this before, but she also knew that with Khan by her side, she could overcome whatever obstacles lay ahead. Her resolve hardened, and she felt the fire of battle ignite once more within her.

"Thank you, Khan," Jessie said, her voice stronger now. "With your help, I know we can do this. For Elsie, for justice, and to protect others from suffering the same fate."

"Indeed, Miss Jessie," Khan said.

As the ferry approached its destination, Jessie felt her doubts recede, replaced by a fierce resolve to see this through to the end. She knew the road ahead would be fraught with danger and uncertainty, but she refused to let fear hold her back. With Khan's guidance and their shared commitment to seeking justice for Elsie, nothing would stand in their way.

Jessie's gaze drifted to the rippling water, its surface glittering like a thousand diamonds under the afternoon sun. She marvelled at the ease with which Khan spoke, and a thought struck her like a bolt of lightning – she had been conversing with a cat as though it were the most natural thing in the world.

"Khan," Jessie said hesitantly, "how is it that I can understand you? It seems... impossible."

"Ah, Miss Jessie, it is because you possess a rare gift," Khan explained, his whiskers twitching with amusement. "You can communicate with beings such as myself and access the paranormal realm. It has been dormant within you for some time, but it appears that your connection with Elsie's passing has awakened this power."

Jessie blinked in astonishment. She had always felt a certain affinity for the strange and inexplicable, but never before had she imagined that she might be a part of that world. Her heart pounded, a mix of excitement and trepidation coursing through her veins.

"Does this mean that together, we can unlock secrets beyond my wildest imagination?" she asked, her voice barely above a whisper.

"Indeed, Miss Jessie," Khan replied, his tail flicking as he observed the wonder in her eyes. "With your newfound abilities and my knowledge of the supernatural, we will make a formidable team."

Jessie could scarcely believe her ears. She had always sought adventure and mystery, but now, she found herself on the precipice of something truly extraordinary. With a deep breath, she reached out a hand to stroke Khan's soft fur, feeling the steady thrum of his purr beneath her fingertips.

"Thank you, Khan," Jessie murmured, her gratitude evident in every word. "I never thought I'd find a friend who shares my fascination with the unknown or who would guide me through it. Together, we'll stand up against the darkness and ensure that Elsie's death was not in vain."

Khan tilted his head and locked his gaze with Jessie's, his green eyes filled with warmth and understanding. "You are most welcome, Miss Jessie," he said softly. "I have no doubt that our partnership will shine a light into the shadows and reveal truths that were once hidden. Let us embark on this journey together, side by side."

Aware of the extraordinary gift that now connected her to Khan, Jessie glanced around the bustling ferry, observing the faces of those who mingled and conversed, entirely oblivious to the supernatural undercurrents that swirled beneath the surface. She felt as if she carried a fragile secret in the palm of her hand, one that could easily shatter if mishandled. At that moment, Jessie came to a decision: their investigation would remain a secret, known only to her and Khan.

"Khan," she whispered, leaning close to the cat's silky black ear, "we mustn't let anyone know about our partnership or my newfound abilities. The shadows that conspire against us may use such knowledge to their advantage and place us both in danger."

"Agreed, Miss Jessie," Khan replied in a soft murmur. "Our bond is precious and unique. It should be kept hidden from prying eyes and malevolent intentions. You have my word that our secret will remain safe with me."

Jessie sighed in relief, feeling the weight of her decision settle around her shoulders like an invisible cloak.

"Where do we even begin, Khan?" Jessie mused, her voice barely audible above the rush of water and hum of conversation.

"First, we must gather information, Miss Jessie," Khan advised, his green eyes narrowing in thought. "We shall start by retracing Elsie's final steps and speaking to those who knew her best."

Jessie nodded. With Khan's guidance, they would piece together the puzzle of Elsie's murder and bring the killer to justice. And though she knew the risks would be great, her single-mindedness burned like a beacon in the night.

"Very well," Jessie said quietly, her words carried away by the wind. "Let's begin our investigation, Khan. Together, we'll expose the truth and ensure that Elsie's killer is brought to justice."

"Indeed, Miss Jessie," Khan agreed, his tail flicking in anticipation. "Our journey will be dangerous but I have no doubt that we shall prevail. After all, our partnership has been forged by fate itself."

The Royal Iris Mersey Ferry

The Royal Iris II Mersey ferry cut through the tidal river, sending white foam swirling around its hull as it steamed towards its destination of New Brighton on the Wirral peninsular opposite the city of Liverpool. The sun cast a golden glow on the river's surface, while the salty breeze whipped around the open promenade deck, carrying the cries of seagulls with it. Passengers milled about, their excited chatter mingling with the distant foghorn and the rhythmic thud of the ferry's engine. Those passengers were unaware of the presence of Khan, the magical, talking black cat.

As the ferry docked and the passengers disembarked, Jessie stepped off the vessel, her eyes scanning the streets for any clue that might lead them closer to solving the mystery. With Khan by her side, they were about to set off on an investigation that would take them deeper into the supernatural realm than either could have ever imagined.

And as they vanished into the throngs of people, the shadows seemed to quiver in their wake, as though sensing the arrival of two determined souls who would stop at nothing to uncover the truth.

STEPPING OFF THE FERRY, Jessie breathed in the bracing sea air, her hair fluttering around her face like a fiery halo. New Brighton's familiar sights and sounds should have brought comfort, but today they only heightened her sense of unease.

As she approached the spot where Elsie's drowned corpse had lain, her emotions threatened to overwhelm her. Elsie, her dear friend, had been cruelly taken from this world. A deck hand on the ferry had seen her pushed overboard by a man wearing a trench coat. Jessie couldn't shake the mental images of her watery fate and her lifeless body. Her hands trembled, betraying her otherwise composed exterior, and a furrowed brow indicated the flurry of thoughts racing through her mind. Blinking back tears that welled up in her eyes, she steeled herself for what lay ahead.

"Miss, are you alright?" a police officer asked, concern etched across his face.

"Fine," she replied curtly, not bothering to mask the quiver in her voice. "Just let me do my job."

"What job may that be?" The officer said.

"Never mind. I have come here to see where my friend was murdered. After that, I need to go to the mortuary to identify her body."

"So, you are a relative then? Sister perhaps?" the officer said.

"Yes, something like that," Jessie muttered and wondered why she had misled the officer.

Ignoring the officer's own mutterings and the concerned stares of passers-by, Jessie knelt beside the chalk outline that marked where Elsie's body had lain after being fished from the water. She swallowed hard, fighting back a fresh wave of tears, but she remained steadfast. She owed it to Elsie to find the truth, no matter how painful the journey would be.

"Talk to me, Elsie," Jessie whispered, closing her eyes and trying to picture the spirited woman who had once filled her days with laughter. "Help me figure out who did this to you."

A gust of wind carried the scent of the nearby fish market toward her, and she couldn't help but think of how Elsie would have made a raucous joke about the smell.

Jessie allowed herself a small smile before refocusing on the task at hand.

"Alright, then," she murmured, wiping away a stray tear with the back of her hand. "Let's get to work."

"Jessie, take a moment. We can do this together," Khan's voice was steady and reassuring as he approached her side. "Do not worry, no one else can see or hear me. I have cast an entrancement barrier around us. No humans can penetrate that barrier."

"Thanks, Khan. I know we can find the truth, but it's just so hard to see Elsie reduced to nothing more than a chalk outline," Jessie admitted her voice tight with emotion. "She deserves better."

"Agreed," Khan nodded solemnly. "But right now, we need to focus on finding the person who did this. Let's start by examining her belongings."

Together, they turned their attention to a small pile of Elsie's personal effects that had been collected from the scene. Among them were her purse, keys, and a broken necklace – its delicate chain snapped in two and several links missing. Jessie picked up the necklace, running her fingers over the remaining links. She knew Elsie had cherished it; it had been a gift from her mother.

"Hey, what's this?" Khan asked, holding up a crumpled piece of paper between his paws. He had found it tucked away in one of the inner pockets of Elsie's purse. He handed it to Jessie and carefully, she unfolded it, revealing a hastily scrawled message: 'Meet me at the docks, 10 pm.'

"Looks like she was meant to meet someone the night she was killed," Jessie murmured, her brow furrowing in thought. "I don't recognise the handwriting though and Elsie never mentioned meeting anyone to me."

Khan shook his head. "But it might be worth looking into. It could be our first real lead."

"Definitely." Jessie stared at the note, her mind racing with possibilities. Despite the heavy weight of grief pressing down on her, she couldn't help but feel a spark of determination ignite within her. She would find the person who had taken Elsie from her, and she would make sure they paid for their crime.

Jessie made sure the police constable was looking away when she said, "Let's start by talking to her colleagues at the council," tucking the note into her pocket for safekeeping. "Maybe someone knows something about this meeting or who she was supposed to see."

"Good idea," Khan agreed, offering a supportive smile. "We'll get to the bottom of this, Jessie. We'll bring justice to Elsie."

Khan remained invisible as Jessie waited for the next ferry returning to Liverpool.

The Council

As Jessie and the invisible Khan walked towards Liverpool's council building, Jessie couldn't help but think that Elsie's spirit was with them, guiding them on their quest for the truth. And with Khan by her side, she knew they would uncover the secrets hidden in the shadows, no matter how dangerous the path became.

The sun dipped low in the sky as Jessie and Khan approached the Liverpool City council building, casting long, ominous shadows on the pavement. The grand façade loomed over them, its ornate stonework a testament to the power and wealth that resided within. As they entered the bustling corridors, filled with suited men and women who hurried about their business, Jessie couldn't help but feel a shiver of unease.

"Jessie," Khan whispered, leaning in close as they walked. "Listen."

Jessie strained her ears and caught snatches of a hushed conversation between two council members just around the corner. Their voices were tense and urgent, laced with a hint of fear.

"...can't keep this up much longer," one of them murmured. "People are starting to ask questions. It's only a matter of time before they find out—"

"Keep your voice down!" the other hissed, glancing nervously around. "We just need to stay calm and stick to the plan. Everything will be fine as long as we don't arouse suspicion."

Jessie exchanged a worried glance with Khan. What were these council members hiding? She felt a wave of anger surge through her. This corruption had to be connected to Elsie's murder somehow, and she vowed to bring it to light.

They continued down the corridor, seeking out Elsie's co-workers. A middle-aged woman named Paula, who had worked closely with Elsie, looked up from her desk as Jessie and Khan approached.

"Hello, Paula," Jessie said softly. "We're trying to find out more about Elsie's murder. Did she ever mention any problems with her colleagues or anyone else here?"

Paula hesitated, chewing on her lip. "Well, there was some tension between Elsie and Councillor Thompson," she admitted finally. "I think they disagreed on a few policy matters, but I didn't think it was anything serious."

"Interesting," Jessie mused, her mind racing. "And did Elsie ever mention meeting someone the night she was killed? Someone outside of work?"

"Actually, yes," Paula replied, her brow furrowing in thought. "She mentioned that she had to meet someone important, but she didn't say who or why. She seemed a bit on edge about it."

"Thank you, Paula," Jessie said gratefully. "This information could be very helpful."

As they left Paula's office, Jessie couldn't help but feel the weight of suspicion growing heavier with each passing moment. The council building, once a familiar and comforting place, now seemed to be hiding dark secrets within its opulent walls. And no matter how dangerous the path became, Jessie knew she wouldn't rest until those secrets were exposed and justice was served for her dear friend Elsie.

"Khan," she whispered, clutching the mysterious note from Elsie's belongings tightly in her hand. "We need to investigate Councillor Thompson and find out more about this meeting. I have a feeling we're getting closer to the truth."

Jessie's heels clicked on the polished marble floors as she and Khan made their way through the opulent halls of the Liverpool City Council. The grandiose building was steeped in history, its walls adorned with oil paintings of stern-faced council members from bygone eras, their eyes seemingly following them as they passed. A thick air of secrecy seemed to hang heavily over the ornate corridors, and Jessie could feel the whispers of hidden agendas reverberating around her.

"Excuse me, Councillor Thompson?" Jessie called out, spotting the man at the far end of the corridor. He stopped abruptly and turned to face her, his face a mixture of surprise and annoyance.

"Yes, miss," he said curtly, attempting to hide his unease as Jessie and Khan approached him. "Who are you and what can I do for you?"

"Actually, I'm an old friend of Elsie's and trying to understand who would want to kill her." Jessie began, her voice steady despite the trembling of her hands, "we wanted to talk to you about her. We've been speaking to some of her colleagues, and your name came up."

"Ah, yes. Elsie." Councillor Thompson's face darkened momentarily before he forced a polite smile. "A tragic loss for us all. But I assure you, Miss ... I had nothing to do with her untimely death."

"Sorry, Harper, Miss Harper, Jessie," she faltered. "Nobody is accusing you of anything, Councillor," she added. "We're just trying to piece together what happened the night she was killed. It's our understanding that you two had some disagreements on policy matters?"

Councillor Thompson's eyes narrowed, and he crossed his arms defensively. "We had our differences, as anyone does in this line of work. But those disagreements were strictly professional. I see no reason why they should be brought into question now."

"Because, Councillor," Jessie said firmly, her determination unwavering, "Elsie mentioned meeting someone important the night she was killed. And we're going to find out who that person was and what they wanted, even if it means uncovering some unsavoury truths about this council."

"Miss Harper," Councillor Thompson warned, his voice low and menacing, "I would advise you not to go digging where you don't belong. The inner workings of this council are far more complex than you could possibly understand."

"Is that a threat, Councillor?" Jessie asked, refusing to back down as she met his gaze head-on.

"Consider it a word of caution and if you have any sense you will leave this business to the police," he said, before turning on his heel and stalking away.

Jessie watched him go, her brow furrowed in concentration. She knew she was wading into dangerous waters, but she had no intention of giving up. Elsie deserved justice, and Jessie would see it done – no matter the cost.

Jessie heard, "Pssst!" She looked up to see Khan entering a room marked 'Archives.' Jessie followed.

"Jessie," Khan whispered, his eyes wide with a mix of shock and disbelief as they stood in a dimly lit corner of the Liverpool City Council's archives room. "Look at this."

In his paws, he held a worn file folder, its edges frayed and discoloured from years of being hidden away. The document inside, however, was far more intriguing. It revealed a connection between Elsie and Councillor Thompson – a series of meetings and payments that suggested a shady partnership.

"Thompson," Jessie murmured, her heart pounding. "I knew there was something wrong about him. But what could Elsie have been involved in?"

"Whatever it is, we need to find more evidence before confronting anyone," Khan said.

Jessie nodded, her thoughts racing as she devised a plan. She'd always been resourceful, able to piece together information and formulate strategies on a whim. This mystery would be no different.

"Alright," she began, her voice low and steady as she shared her thoughts with Khan. "We'll split up. I'll head to the council members' offices and look for any hidden documents or correspondence. You eavesdrop on conversations among the staff and see if you can pick up any clues about Elsie's involvement with Thompson. Best make yourself invisible though."

"Sounds good," Khan agreed. They both knew the importance of discretion in their investigation; the last thing they needed was to alert the council to their suspicions.

The pair went their separate ways, moving silently through the opulent corridors adorned with portraits of past council members, each one staring down at them with an air of secret knowledge. Jessie couldn't shake the feeling that the walls themselves were whispering, sharing hidden agendas and long-buried secrets.

As she approached the council members' offices, Jessie noticed a cleaner's trolley left unattended in the hallway. Seizing the opportunity, she grabbed a pair of rubber gloves and slipped them on, hoping to avoid leaving any trace of her presence.

Carefully, she entered the first office. Her heart raced as she searched through drawers, cabinets, and shelves, seeking any hint of Elsie's connection to Thompson or the council's shady dealings. Though she found nothing concrete, Jessie couldn't help but notice that several documents were stamped with a mysterious symbol – an insignia she'd never seen before. Could it be a clue?

Meanwhile, Khan had positioned himself near a group of junior clerical staff, who were chatting animatedly during their lunch break. He strained to hear their conversation, hoping to catch any mention of Elsie or Thompson. As he listened, one woman's voice rose above the others, tinged with worry.

"Have you heard the rumours about Councillor Thompson?" she asked nervously. "I don't want to believe them, but after what happened to Elsie..."

Khan's ears perked up at the mention of their names. This was exactly what they needed – proof that there was more to Elsie's murder than met the eye and that others within the council suspected something sinister was at play.

As Jessie and Khan continued their covert investigation, they knew they were edging closer to the truth. They would not stop until they'd uncovered the web of deceit woven throughout the Liverpool City Council.

Jessie and Khan met up again at the end of a long corridor but found themselves at a locked door, the brass doorknob gleaming under the dim, flickering light. Jessie's brow furrowed as she weighed their options. They couldn't turn back now; they were so close to finding more evidence.

"Let me try," Khan whispered, casting a spell over the lock. He had always been resourceful in unexpected ways, much to Jessie's surprise and appreciation. As he crouched down and began his incantations, Jessie kept watch, her heart pounding like a hammer against an anvil.

"Come on, come on," Jessie muttered under her breath, clenching her fists at her sides. The silence was shattered by the sudden sound of footsteps echoing through the corridor—someone was approaching.

"Got it!" Khan exclaimed just as the door cracked open. Jessie quickly pulled him into the room, closing the door behind them with a soft click.

"Phew, that was close," Khan panted.

Jessie scanned the room, a luxurious office filled with leather-bound books and expensive trinkets, every inch exuding power and influence. She felt a wave of disgust wash over her; how many secrets lay hidden behind these opulent walls?

"Let's hurry up and see if we can find anything useful," Jessie said, determination burning in her eyes. They searched the room meticulously, sifting through piles of documents and rifling through drawers.

As Khan inspected a dusty bookshelf, Jessie overheard muffled voices coming from the corridor outside. Pressing her ear to the door, she strained to make out the words, her heart racing with anticipation.

"...can't let anyone find out about this," one voice hissed, sounding agitated. "If it gets out, it'll ruin everything."

"Relax," another voice replied, smooth and confident. "No one will ever know. Elsie was the only one who could've exposed us, but she's no longer a problem."

Jessie felt her blood run cold at the mention of Elsie. A blistering rage bubbled up inside her, fuelling her desire to uncover the truth behind her friend's murder.

"Khan," Jessie whispered, her voice shaking with emotion. "I just overheard something... I think we're on to something."

In the dimly lit room of the council building, Jessie's mind wandered to her childhood fascination with the paranormal. She had spent countless nights reading ghost stories and hunting for spirits in the old cemetery near her home. It was a passion that had followed her into adulthood, leading to an interest in solving mysteries beyond the veil. But now, as she stood in this opulent den of corruption, she realised that sometimes, the most horrifying monsters were not supernatural at all – they hid in plain sight, disguised as respectable citizens.

"Jessie, come look at this," Khan called out, breaking her reverie. He pawed at a crumpled piece of paper, his brow furrowed in concentration.

"Is it a clue?" Jessie asked, her voice barely above a whisper as she took the note from him.

"Could be," Khan said. "It's a list of names, including Elsie's, and some cryptic notes about 'payments' and 'silence.' We need to find out who these people are and what their connection is to Elsie."

"Right," Jessie agreed, her green eyes blazing with strength of character. "Let's get to work."

As they pored over the list, Jessie couldn't help but wonder how deep this web of deceit went. Were there other victims like Elsie, caught in the middle of a deadly power play? And could she and Khan expose the truth before more lives were lost?

"Hey, Jessie, look at this," Khan said, pointing at a name on the list. "This one works in the finance department. Maybe they know something about these 'payments.'"

"Good idea," Jessie nodded, tucking the note into her pocket. "Let's go talk to them."

They made their way through the labyrinthine halls of the council building, passing under the watchful gaze of stern portraits and ornate chandeliers. Jessie felt a shiver run down her spine as she realised the weight of their discovery; it was like walking through a haunted house, aware that the ghosts were still very much alive.

"Jessie," Khan said quietly, "we'll get to the bottom of this, I promise."

"Thank you, Khan," Jessie replied, swallowing hard. "I just can't believe Elsie was caught up in all of this."

"Nobody does," Khan agreed, "but we're going to make sure no one else gets hurt."

As they approached the finance department, Jessie steeled herself for the confrontation ahead. The air was thick with tension, and she knew that every step forward brought them closer not only to the truth but also to potential danger.

"Here goes nothing," Jessie whispered, pushing open the door to the finance department. Little did they know, the department's records held the key to uncovering one piece of the puzzle - one that people would kill for to keep secret.

Help

The Kardomah café in Dale Street hummed with the comforting, familiar sounds of daily life. A symphony of porcelain cups and saucers clinked as they met their respective resting places on table tops, while the hiss and gurgle of the espresso machine punctuated the air. The scent of freshly brewed coffee wafted through the room, mingling with the sweet aroma of buttery pastries that had just been pulled from the oven. Hushed voices murmured in the background, creating an atmosphere that was at once soothing and alive.

Jessie sat in a cosy corner, her hands wrapped around a warm teacup as she waited for George Jenkins to arrive. Nervous anticipation bubbled inside her like the frothy milk atop her coffee cup, causing her fingers to fidget with the delicate cup handle. She tried to distract herself from the steam swirling up from the creamy liquid, but her mind couldn't help but race back to George, wondering how much he might have changed since their school days.

"Come on, Jessie," she muttered to herself, "you're not a nervous schoolgirl anymore." She took a deep breath, inhaling the rich aromas of the coffee shop and willed her heart to slow its frantic pace.

As she glanced around the café, her eyes fell on a couple engaged in hushed conversation, heads bent towards each other as if sharing a precious secret. Jessie couldn't help but feel a pang of envy, hoping that she and George would be able to rekindle that same closeness they had once shared.

"Focus," Jessie admonished herself, taking another sip of her coffee and trying to still her racing thoughts. She knew she had far more important matters at hand – the investigation into Elsie's murder weighed heavily on her mind, casting a shadow over the excitement of her reunion with George.

With each tick of the clock, Jessie's anticipation grew, her fingers tightening around the teacup, her eyes flitting to the door every time it opened. She knew that George had his own battle scars, both physical and emotional, but she couldn't shake the hope that their meeting would bring something positive into both their lives.

"Please let this work," she whispered under her breath, a silent plea for the universe to grant them a chance at rekindling their lost friendship. As she took another sip of her coffee, she couldn't help but imagine what lay in store for her and George as they embarked on this dangerous journey together.

The door to the café swung open, and in walked George Jenkins. He was a distinguished-looking man with dark hair neatly combed back, a trimmed moustache that lent him an air of sophistication, and dark brown eyes like molten chocolate that seemed to take in everything around him. Dressed impeccably in a well-tailored suit and wearing a black homburg, he carried himself with confidence despite the slight limp in his step – a lasting reminder of the war that had left its mark on both his body and soul. As he approached Jessie's table, leaning on his cane for support, she couldn't help but be struck by how much he had changed since their school days together.

"George!" she exclaimed, her voice tinged with excitement as she rose to greet him. "It's been so long – you look wonderful."

"Jessie," George replied warmly, his eyes crinkling at the corners as he smiled. "You haven't changed a bit. Still as lovely as ever." He extended his hand, which she took gratefully, feeling the reassuring grip of his fingers around hers.

"Please, sit down," Jessie gestured to the empty seat opposite her, watching as George carefully lowered himself into the chair with the aid of his cane. As he settled in, she couldn't help but wonder what had transpired during the years they had spent apart, to mould him into the man seated before her now.

"Thank you for agreeing to meet me," Jessie began, trying to quell the fluttering in her stomach. "I wasn't sure if you'd remember me from our schooldays."

"Of course, I remember you, our families were quite close, weren't they?" George chuckled, his eyes twinkling with amusement. "We may have lost touch, but I could never forget our misadventures together. You were always such a spirited young lady – it seems some things never change."

Jessie blushed at his words, remembering the scrapes they used to get into as children. "Well, we've certainly grown up since then, haven't we?" she said with a small smile.

"Indeed," George agreed, his gaze turning thoughtful. "Time has a way of changing all things – sometimes for the better, sometimes not. But I must say, it's been a pleasure to see you again after all these years."

"Likewise," Jessie replied, her heart swelling with gratitude for this unexpected reunion. As they exchanged pleasantries and reminisced about their shared past, she felt an inexplicable sense of comfort in his presence – as if the years apart had never happened. As they delved deeper into the conversation, Jessie found herself growing more and more intrigued by the man George had become, her curiosity piqued by the hints of a life filled with adventure and intrigue.

"Speaking of change," George began, his eyes narrowing with genuine concern, "I heard about your friend Elsie. I'm terribly sorry, Jessie." He reached across the table to give her hand a gentle squeeze.

"Thank you, George," Jessie murmured, touched by his sincerity. She hesitated for a moment before asking, "How did you come to know about it?"

"Word spreads quickly in this town, especially when it comes to something as tragic as murder. And in my line of work, well, let's just say I hear things others might not," he explained, his voice lowering conspiratorially.

"Your line of work?" Jessie asked, curious about what George had been up to all these years.

"Ah, yes," he replied, running a hand through his hair. "I work as a CID Admin clerk with Liverpool City Police. I've always had an interest in criminal investigations, and though I may be stuck behind a desk, I've managed to learn a thing or two about navigating the city's hidden corners."

"Really?" Jessie's eyes widened, intrigued by George's unexpected expertise. "That must come in handy."

"Indeed, it does," he agreed, leaning in closer. "For instance, I've heard whispers about a certain criminal underbelly in Liverpool – one that most people don't even know exists. It's fascinating, really, how much goes on beneath the surface. But enough about me," George said, waving off his own accomplishments. "Tell me more about Elsie. What have you discovered in your investigation so far?"

Jessie hesitated, weighing the pros and cons of revealing her involvement in the case. But something in George's earnest gaze convinced her that she could trust him – that perhaps his experience and connections could prove invaluable in solving Elsie's murder. And so, she took a deep breath and began to share the details of her investigation with him.

As Jessie spoke, George listened intently, his eyes sharp and his mind working tirelessly to piece together the puzzle before them. He asked thoughtful questions, probing for more information on suspects, motives, and any clues that might lead them closer to the truth. As their conversation progressed, Jessie couldn't help but feel a sense of camaraderie with George – a partnership forged in their mutual quest for justice.

"Jessie," George said suddenly, his expression serious, "I want you to know that I'm here to help you in any way I can. If my connections or knowledge can aid your investigation, please don't hesitate to ask."

"Thank you, George," Jessie replied, her voice thick with gratitude. As they sat there in the cosy corner of the café, surrounded by the comforting aroma of fresh coffee and the soft murmur of conversation, she knew she had found a valuable ally in her pursuit of the truth. Together, they were steadfast in their desire to find Elsie's killer – no matter where the investigation led them.

Despite George's earnest offer of help, Jessie hesitated. She couldn't deny the value of his expertise and connections, but the thought of involving him in her dangerous investigation was unsettling. Her fingers tapped nervously against the cup, betraying her inner turmoil.

"George," she began, her voice wavering, "I appreciate your willingness to help, truly. But I don't want to put you at risk. This case... it appears to have a dark side."

"Jessie, I understand your concern." He placed a reassuring hand on hers, stilling her tapping fingers. "But I can handle myself. I've had my share of close calls over the years."

"I'm sure you have," she said, unconvinced. "But this is different, George. And I couldn't live with myself if something happened to you because of my investigation."

"Then let me share something with you," he said, leaning back in his chair, his eyes far away as he recalled a memory from his past. "A while back, I found myself entangled in a particularly nasty case. On paper, I was just an admin clerk, but I couldn't get the details out of my head. So, I started digging deeper on my own – late nights, following leads no one else bothered to pursue."

Jessie listened intently as George recounted how he'd managed to infiltrate a hidden gambling den that had been connected to several unsolved cases. His resourcefulness and cunning had not only led him to uncover crucial evidence but also brought about the eventual arrest of a notorious crime boss.

"Though it was risky, and I was going against the grain, I knew deep down that I couldn't stand idly by," George continued, his voice firm with conviction. "That same determination, Jessie, is what I'll bring to your investigation. We're both after the same thing – justice for Elsie."

Jessie's brow furrowed as she mulled over George's story, her uncertainty slowly giving way to a newfound appreciation for his tenacity. If he had managed to navigate such treacherous waters before, then perhaps she could trust him with her own investigation.

"Alright, George," she finally said, locking eyes with him. "Let's do this together. But please, promise me one thing: if it ever gets too dangerous, you'll step back. I can't have your blood on my hands."

"Deal," he agreed, offering her a firm handshake that solidified their partnership. "Now, let's get started."

"George, I have to admit," Jessie began, hesitating for a moment before continuing. "I've been trying to piece together this mystery on my own, but there's only so much I can do. Your knowledge of the city's criminal underworld could be invaluable." She looked at him with a mixture of curiosity and admiration.

"Jessie, I'd be honoured to help you find Elsie's killer," George replied, a fierce glint in his eyes. "But it's not just about my connections or experience. It's about working together as a team, using our strengths to uncover the truth."

Jessie found herself nodding in agreement, struck by the sincerity in George's voice. She knew that she was far from an expert in navigating the darker corners of Liverpool, but perhaps with George's guidance, she could become the investigator she needed to be. Her heart swelled with anticipation at the prospect of their collaboration.

"Alright then," Jessie said, her voice steady and resolute. "Let's start by discussing what we already know about Elsie's murder and see if anything stands out as a potential lead."

"Good idea," George agreed, leaning in closer as they began to piece together the facts of the case. They discussed the known details, each contributing their own insights and observations. It wasn't long before they discovered a possible connection that had previously eluded Jessie.

"Wait a minute," George said suddenly, his face lighting up with excitement. "This person – could they be involved somehow?"

Jessie considered the new information, her mind racing with possibilities. "It's worth looking into," she conceded, feeling a fresh surge of hope. "But we'll need to tread carefully. If they are connected to Elsie's murder, who knows what they're capable of?"

"Agreed," George said, his eyes narrowing as he mulled over their next steps. "But we're in this together now, Jessie. And I promise you, we won't rest until we find the truth."

With that, their newfound partnership was solidified, and they began to plan their next move. Little did they know what twists and turns awaited them. But one thing was certain: together, Jessie and George would leave no stone unturned in their pursuit of justice for Elsie.

As Jessie and George exchanged ideas, the corner of the café seemed to shrink around them, transforming into a clandestine meeting place where secrets were shared and alliances forged. The aroma of coffee and the low hum of conversation faded into the background, leaving only the quest that bound them together.

"George," Jessie began, her voice steady and resolute, "we must be prepared for anything. This investigation could lead us down some dark paths, and there's no telling what we'll uncover."

He nodded in agreement. "I know, Jessie. But I'm ready for whatever tests lie ahead. And from what I've seen today, you're more than capable of handling yourself."

A warm feeling washed over Jessie, as she felt both reassured by and grateful for George's unwavering support. At the same time, a sense of foreboding settled within her – a nagging reminder of the unknown dangers that lay waiting in the shadows of Liverpool's criminal underworld.

"I have a feeling this is just the beginning," she whispered, her fingers tightening around the porcelain teacup. "Once we start pulling at these threads, who knows what we'll unravel?"

"True, but we won't be unravelling them alone," George reminded her with a reassuring smile. "Together, we stand a much better chance of solving this mystery."

Jessie returned his smile. At that moment, she knew they were embarking on an extraordinary journey – one filled with danger, deception, and possibly even betrayal. But with George by her side, she felt confident that they would weather every storm and eventually unearth the truth.

"Then let's begin our partnership here and now," she said, extending her hand across the table. George grasped it firmly, sealing their alliance with a sense of anticipation and excitement that was almost palpable.

"Here's to new beginnings, Jessie," he said, his voice tinged with equal parts hope and determination. "And to the many discoveries that lie ahead."

As they released their hands and settled back into their seats, the murmur of the café slowly returned to the forefront of their awareness, like a world waking up around them. As Jessie looked into George's eyes – filled with the promise of adventure, camaraderie, and righting wrongs – she couldn't help but feel that their partnership was destined for greatness.

"Here's to us, George," she replied softly, raising her cup in a silent toast. "And to the mysteries we'll solve together."

Little did they know just how soon those words would be put to the test.

The following morning, Jessie awoke with the first light of dawn, her mind racing with both excitement and trepidation. She sat up in bed and wrapped her dressing gown around her, the crisp autumn air sending a shiver down her spine. From her window, she saw the sun peeking above the horizon, casting a soft golden glow on the quiet streets below. It was a fresh start, not only for the day but also for her partnership with George.

"Today's the day," she murmured to herself, steeling herself as she prepared to face whatever lay ahead.

Jessie had always been a woman of action, so she wasted no time getting ready for the day. She dressed quickly, opting for a simple yet elegant blouse and skirt that would allow her to move freely during their investigation. As she pinned her auburn hair into a neat chignon, she caught a glimpse of herself in the mirror and couldn't help but smile. There was a fire in her eyes that hadn't been there before – a spark ignited by the prospect of working alongside someone as capable and single-minded as George, not to mention the formidable Khan.

"Right then," she said, taking a deep breath and stepping out of her flat, "Let's see what this partnership can do."

When Jessie arrived at the pre-arranged meeting spot, George was already waiting for her, leaning against the brick wall of a nearby building. His cane was held casually in one hand, while the other clutched a paper bag that emitted the tantalising aroma of freshly made bacon sandwiches. He looked every bit the dashing detective, his posture exuding confidence despite the slight limp that betrayed his wounded leg.

"Morning, Jessie," he greeted her with a grin, offering her the bag. "Thought we could use some sustenance before we dive headfirst into our investigation."

"Thank you, George," she replied, accepting the bag and peering inside. "They smell divine, just what we need to keep our energy up."

As they walked side by side, Jessie couldn't help but feel a sense of camaraderie with George that she hadn't experienced in a long time. They chatted amiably about their plans for the day, discussing potential leads and sharing their theories on Elsie's murder case. It was clear from their conversation that George's keen intellect and extensive knowledge of Liverpool's criminal underworld would be invaluable assets in their investigation.

"George," Jessie began, her voice tinged with curiosity, "how did you come to know so much about this city's darker corners?"

"Ah," he said with a wry smile, "that's a story for another time, perhaps when we're not knee-deep in a murder case."

"Fair enough," she conceded, her interest piqued but respecting his desire for privacy. "I suppose we should focus on the task at hand."

As they delved deeper into the heart of Liverpool, following leads and questioning witnesses, Jessie found herself increasingly impressed by George's resourcefulness. He seemed to have a knack for drawing out information from even the most tight-lipped individuals, using both charm and tact to persuade them to speak. And as they pieced together the puzzle of Elsie's murder, it became apparent that their partnership was a force to be reckoned with.

"Jessie," George said after a particularly fruitful interview with a reluctant witness, "I have to say, I'm thoroughly enjoying working alongside you. You have an incredible talent for reading people and getting to the truth."

"Thank you," she replied, touched by his compliment. "I could say the same about you, George. Together, I think we can solve anything."

"Perhaps you are right, Jessie, but permit me to arrange a discreet meeting with Detective Sergeant Bill Roberts of the Hatton Garden CID."

"Nothing ventured... as they say. I trust your judgement," Jessie said.

More Help

THE DIMLY LIT PUB was filled with a dense cloud of smoke, which hung heavily in the air as Jessie and George entered. The low murmur of hushed voices echoed throughout the small space, with patrons leaning in to speak conspiratorially to one another. It was the perfect place for discreet conversations, and they knew that Detective Sergeant Bill Roberts would be no exception.

"Over there," George whispered, nodding towards a man sitting alone in the corner booth. He led Jessie through the maze of tables, her auburn hair shimmering under the flickering lights as she moved gracefully across the room. Despite her lack of an accent and knowledge of the fishwives' bawdy lexicon, she blended seamlessly into the eclectic crowd in a typical Liverpool Sailor's Town pub.

"Evening, Bill," George greeted him with a smile as they slid into the booth across from him. He raised his glass in acknowledgement, his dark eyes narrowing as he studied their faces. There was nothing about his expression that suggested he'd been expecting them.

"Jessie, George," he replied, his tone cautious. "First of all, let me say it's a pleasure to meet you. George speaks highly of you."

"Thank you," Jessie said blushing.

Bill continued, "I've been hearing some whispers about corruption lately. Things aren't quite adding up in this city, and I think it traces back to the council."

"Corruption?" George asked, his brow furrowing in concern. "That's quite the accusation."

"Things have changed since the old days" Bill said, running a hand through his receding hair. "I didn't get to where I am by turning a blind eye. It's not just about lining their pockets anymore – people are getting hurt."

"Are you saying there's a connection between the corruption and Elsie's murder?" Jessie inquired, her hazel eyes flashing with curiosity. She had been unable to shake the feeling that there was more to the story, and now it seemed as though her instincts were proving correct.

"I don't know yet," Bill admitted, taking a swig from his pint. "But I'm willing to bet that there is. If we dig deep enough, we might just uncover the truth."

Jessie's heart pounded as she processed the information. She knew the stakes were high and the road ahead would be dangerous, but she couldn't ignore the injustice any longer. Glancing at George, she found him staring intently at Bill, the gears turning in his head.

"Alright then," Jessie said firmly, her voice barely audible above the chatter of the pub. "Let's get to work."

Jessie leaned in closer, her elbows resting on the worn wooden table as she spoke. "I've been digging into Elsie's murder, and there's a potential connection to a secret society."

"Secret society?" Bill raised an eyebrow, his interest piqued. "Go on."

"During my research, I stumbled upon a symbol –" Jessie pulled out a folded piece of paper from her purse, unfolding it carefully to reveal a sketch of an intricate emblem. "This was found at the scene where Elsie was killed. It's the same symbol associated with a group called The Circle of Shadows. They're rumoured to have strong ties to the city council, though no one seems to know much about their activities."

George studied the sketch intently, his brow furrowed in concentration. He glanced up, meeting Jessie's gaze. "You think this group had something to do with Elsie's murder?"

"Perhaps," Jessie replied, her eyes flicking to Bill for validation. "But of course, that's just a theory."

"An interesting one," Bill mused, rubbing his chin thoughtfully. "Especially given what I found during my own investigation."

"What's that?" Jessie asked, curiosity dancing in her eyes.

"Over the past few months, there have been several other murders in Liverpool with striking similarities to Elsie's case. All victims were found with the same symbol etched nearby, and each had some sort of connection to the city council."

Jessie felt a chill run down her spine, the gravity of the situation settling upon her like a heavy cloak. She suddenly became aware of the hum of conversation around them, the clink of glasses and the laughter of patrons, all oblivious to the dark conspiracy they were discussing.

"Are you saying there's a pattern to these murders?" George questioned, his voice barely above a whisper.

"Quite possibly," Bill nodded, his gaze serious. "And if that's the case, then we're dealing with something much larger than just corruption within the city council."

"Then we have to stop them," Jessie said firmly, her determination unwavering. She could feel the weight of responsibility on her shoulders but she had never been one to shy away from a challenge.

"Agreed," Bill said in that unmistakeable Welsh accent, his eyes meeting hers with equal doggedness. "Together, we'll uncover the truth and root out those behind these misdeeds."

As they sat in the corner of the pub, united by their shared purpose, Jessie couldn't help but think about the road ahead. It would be treacherous and fraught with danger, but with George and Bill by her side, she felt a sense of hope. They were an unlikely trio. Bill, is a real detective. George, a frustrated detective, and Jessie, a librarian. But each brings their own unique skills and insights to the table.

In the end, it didn't matter where the investigation led them, or what obstacles they faced. What mattered was that they were in this together, and nothing – not even the shadowy tendrils of a secret society – could stand in their way.

The low hum of conversation and the smoky warmth of the pub enveloped Jessie, George, and Bill as they huddled together in a secluded booth. The peculiar lighting cast their faces in shifting shadows, emphasising the gravity of their mission. Jessie absently traced the froth on her glass, her thoughts in turmoil.

"Look," she began, her voice steady despite her nerves, "if we're going to get to the bottom of this, we'll need more than just the three of us. We need allies who can help us navigate the criminal underworld – people with connections and resources."

"Agreed," George chimed in, his brow furrowed in thought. "It's not just about solving Elsie's murder anymore. We're dealing with something much bigger. And we can't do it alone."

Jessie locked eyes with Bill, searching for any hint of hesitation. She knew he had reservations about digging too deep, but to her relief, he simply nodded. "You're right, Jessie. We'll need all the help we can get. I may have some reliable connections within the police force that could be useful."

"Are you sure, Bill?" Jessie asked, concern lacing her words. "I don't want to put you in any danger."

"Neither do I," George added, his face tight with worry.

Bill chuckled softly, a glint in his eyes. "We're already in danger, my friends. But if we don't stand up to this corruption, who will? Besides, I didn't become a detective sergeant to sit idly by while innocent lives are taken."

Jessie couldn't help but admire Bill's grit. As she glanced at George, she saw the same admiration mirrored in his expression. They were an unlikely team, but somehow, it felt like fate had thrown them together.

"Alright then," Jessie said, taking a deep breath. "We'll need a plan. We'll have to be discreet and cautious in our investigation. And most importantly, we have to trust each other."

"Absolutely," George agreed, his hand reaching across the table to grasp Jessie's and Bill's. The warmth of their hands intertwined filled Jessie with newfound hope.

"Let's do this," Bill said, his voice resolute. "Together, we'll bring justice to Elsie and all those who've suffered at the hands of this secret society."

As they sat there, united by their unwavering commitment to uncovering the truth, Jessie felt a strange mix of trepidation and exhilaration coursing through her veins. She knew the path they were embarking on would be riddled with danger and uncertainty, but with George and Bill by her side, she couldn't imagine facing it any other way.

"Then it's settled," Jessie declared, as she gazed at George and Bill, both nodding their agreement. "We'll work together to bring justice to the victims, trusting one another implicitly."

"Partnership it is," Bill confirmed with a half-smile, his eyes reflecting a steely determination. "Now, let me fill you in on the other murders."

As the trio huddled closer around the dimly lit table, Jessie couldn't help but feel an odd sense of camaraderie forming between them. They were a motley crew – her own background steeped in Liverpool's working-class grit, George, a WW I veteran, with his disarming charm and appetite for adventure, and Bill – the seasoned detective sergeant with a drive for truth and doing the right thing.

"Over the past six months," Bill began in a low tone, "there have been three other murders bearing striking similarities to Elsie's. All victims were women in their thirties, each found with peculiar symbols cut into their skin."

Jessie fought off a shudder at the mention of the symbols. Images of Elsie's lifeless body flashed through her mind, and she steeled herself against the wave of grief threatening to consume her.

"Where were they found?" George asked, his brow furrowed in concern.

"Two of them were discovered in abandoned buildings near the docks," Bill replied, his voice heavy with emotion. "The third was found in an alleyway not far from here."

"Any suspects?" Jessie inquired, attempting to keep her voice steady despite the growing unease gnawing at her insides.

"None that have held up to scrutiny," Bill admitted, rubbing his temples wearily. "But there's one lead I've been chasing – a man known only as The Hawk. He's rumoured to be involved with the criminal underworld and has been spotted at the scenes of the murders shortly after they occurred."

"Sounds like someone we should keep an eye on," George noted, his eyes narrowing in thought.

"Agreed," Jessie concurred, her mind racing with possibilities. "We'll need to find out more about him and how he connects to the society."

As Bill detailed the profiles of the other victims, Jessie's goals only intensified. The lives of these women had been cruelly snuffed out, and their families were left to pick up the shattered pieces. She vowed to herself that she would not rest until the truth was uncovered.

"Remember, we're treading dangerous waters here," Bill reminded them, his voice tinged with caution. "We must be vigilant and discreet at all times."

Jessie locked eyes with both George and Bill, sensing the gravity of their shared mission. They were bound by a common goal – to shine a light onto the darkest corners of Liverpool's underbelly and expose the malignant force preying upon innocent lives.

"Understood," she said firmly, her heart swelling with purpose. "Together, we'll put an end to this reign of terror."

The dim lighting of the pub cast flickering shadows on the worn wooden table, as Jessie and George huddled over their hastily scribbled notes. Their heads bowed conspiratorially close together, they attempted to make sense of the tangled web of information Bill had provided them.

"Look here," Jessie said, her hair falling forward as she pointed to a section of her notes. "All the victims were found near the docks – could that be significant?"

"Maybe," George mused, rubbing his chin thoughtfully. "But it's Liverpool, there's bound to be some connection to the water. What about this?" He tapped another part of the notes. "Each woman had a locket with an unusual symbol. That has to tie them to the secret society somehow."

As Jessie studied the rough sketch of the symbol George had drawn, a chill ran down her spine. It was eerily similar to the one she had discovered at Elsie's crime scene. She knew deep in her bones that they were onto something and on the way to solving this grisly puzzle.

"Alright then," she said, her voice low and steady. "We need to find out more about these lockets and what they mean. But we have to be careful. If this society catches wind of our investigation, we could be putting ourselves in danger."

"Yes," George replied, his eyes meeting hers with a solemn understanding. "Discretion is key. We can't let anyone outside of our circle know what we're up to. We'll have to navigate these murky waters without stirring up too much attention."

Jessie mulled over George's words, her mind racing with potential strategies and plans. She knew all too well the power of rumours and whispers within the tight-knit community of Liverpool. One wrong move and their investigation could be compromised.

"Right," she said resolutely, turning her attention back to the notes. "We'll need to devise a plan for gathering information without raising suspicion. Maybe we can enlist some trusted friends to help us keep our ears to the ground."

"Good idea," George agreed, his face lighting up with enthusiasm. "And I'll see what I can dig up on The Hawk and his connections to the criminal underworld. If he's involved in these murders, then maybe he can lead us to what we are looking for."

"Let's do it," Jessie said, her eyes flashing. "Together, we'll find the truth and bring these monsters to justice."

Jessie's gaze lingered on the frothy remnants of her drink, the bubbles popping one by one like a slow countdown. She knew they had to part ways soon, but there was something she needed to say first.

"Bill," Jessie began, her voice tinged with genuine gratitude, "I just want to thank you for your help and expertise. We couldn't do this without you."

A slight blush crept up Bill's cheeks as he scratched the back of his head, clearly uncomfortable with the praise. "It's nothing really, Jessie. I'm just doing my job, trying to make things right."

"Still," George chimed in, a sincere smile tugging at the corners of his mouth. "We appreciate it more than you know."

"Right then," Bill said, clearing his throat and looking away to hide his emotions. "Let's get going, shall we?"

As they stood up from their table, Jessie noticed the way the dim light from the stained-glass windows danced across the pub floor, casting shadows that seemed to mimic the hidden world they were about to delve into. The air around them felt charged with anticipation, thick with the unspoken promise of danger and intrigue.

With a nod to each other, the trio stepped out of the cosy warmth of the pub and into the biting chill of the Liverpool night. As the door closed behind them, Jessie shivered involuntarily, her breath visible in the cold air. It wasn't just the temperature that caused her unease - she knew that the path they were embarking upon was a perilous journey, and yet she couldn't deny the thrill that coursed through her veins.

"Alright," Jessie murmured, mostly to herself, as Bill Roberts went his separate way. "We've got work to do."

Despite the darkness that enveloped them, there was an undeniable glimmer of hope in their eyes. They were bent on discovering the truth. As Jessie and George made their way down the cobblestone streets, a fierce resolution settled over Jessie's entire being.

"Let's show them they messed with the wrong people," she whispered into the night, her voice carried away by the wind as they disappeared into the shadows.

Jessie's heels clicked against the cobblestones as she and George made their way to a tram stop. The faint glow of gas lamps flickered ominously, casting eerie shadows on damp streets and pavement. Jessie could feel the dampness seeping into her bones but she hardly noticed. Her mind was consumed by Bill's revelations and the chilling prospect of a secret society operating within their city.

"Alright," Jessie began, her voice steady despite the whirlwind of thoughts inside her head. "We've got some solid leads from Bill, but we need to dig deeper. What do you think our next move should be, George?"

The night air was crisp, causing George to pull his coat tighter around him as he pondered Jessie's question. He had always been a man of action, and this mystery excited him more than anything else in recent memory.

"First things first," George replied, with a gleam in his eyes. "There is no point in revisiting the scene of Elsie's murder. It was on the ferry but there may be something in her home that could help the investigation."

Jessie nodded, auburn curls bouncing with the motion. She knew George was right; they needed to examine every detail, no matter how small. "Agreed. But we'll have to be discreet. If there's a secret society involved, they'll be watching – and we can't afford to alarm them."

"Right." George rubbed his hands together, the friction creating a fleeting warmth amidst the chill. "We'll have to blend in, maybe even adopt some disguises. We don't want anyone recognising us while we're snooping around."

Jessie smiled at George's enthusiasm, his excitement almost infectious. She imagined them dressed in disguise, mingling with the city's underbelly, and felt a thrill of anticipation. "Disguises it is, then. We'll find some suitable outfits tomorrow."

"Perfect." George's eyes twinkled with a mischievous glint. "Now, let's talk about our allies. We'll need to be careful who we trust, but there are people in this city who might be willing to help us – for the right price, of course."

"True," Jessie mused, her fingers tracing the outline of a nearby bench as they walked. "We'll have to be cautious, though. The moment we start asking questions, we risk exposing ourselves."

"Agreed," George responded, his voice firm. "We'll have to make sure we approach the right people and keep our true intentions hidden."

As they continued strategising, their minds full of possibilities, the wind whispered through the trees overhead, carrying a secret message that only they could decipher. They were determined to unveil the truth behind these murders, and with Bill's help, they had found their starting point.

The Other Crime Scenes

ONCE MORE AT HOME, Jessie's auburn curls framed her serious expression as she leaned forward, hands flat against the surface of the table. "Khan," she said, looking at her cat. "We've got to visit the crime scenes of these other connected murders. There must be something we're missing that ties them all together."

Khan nodded, his eyes narrowing with concern. "It's not just about solving Elsie's murder anymore," he said solemnly. "We need to find the truth for all the victims and their families. They deserve it."

"Absolutely," agreed Jessie, her fists clenching on the table. "And there's always the chance we might prevent further atrocities" she added.

"All right, then," Jessie said, straightening up and looking at the feline. "Let's get to work. But remember, Khan, only I can hear you talk unless we agree on something different and that time has not yet arrived."

As a rendezvous and by prior arrangement, Jessie, George, and Bill met inside the Kardomah café on Dale Street. Khan was there too but had used his powers to cloak himself in invisibility.

As they left the café and made their way toward the first crime scene, Jessie's mind raced with thoughts and theories. She knew she could rely on her keen observation skills to pick up any clues or details others might miss, but she also knew the importance of teamwork. Each member of the group brought their own unique abilities and insights to the table, and Jessie felt a sense of pride in the camaraderie they had built.

"Remember," Jessie said, her voice focused, "we're in this together. If you see something, say something."

The sun had dipped below the horizon as Jessie, George, Bill and the invisible Khan approached the first crime scene. Gloom enshrouded the dimly lit alleyway near the Albert Dock, where shadows pooled in every corner, concealing secrets that the darkness seemed reluctant to give up. The cawing of distant seagulls mingled with the sound of waves lapping against the dock walls, creating an eerie soundtrack for their investigation.

"Jessie," whispered Khan, his voice strained with unease. "Something is unnerving about this place."

Jessie had lingered behind the others in case Khan needed to speak and she needed to reply. "Stay close," she replied, her eyes darting around the alleyway as they ventured further in. Jessie could feel the atmosphere pressing in on her. It was as if the very air were charged with the lingering residue of fear and malice that clung to this place like a shroud.

"Look at this," Jessie said, her voice barely above a whisper as she gestured toward the spot where the murder had occurred. Her companions gathered around her, studying the ground intently.

"Seems like any other alleyway to me," muttered Bill, trying to mask his unease.

"Ah, but is it?" Jessie said, a hint of excitement in her voice. She pointed to a strange symbol etched into the wall just above the ground. It appeared to have been made with a knife or some other sharp object and its jagged lines seemed to pulse with a dark energy of their own.

"Any idea what that means?" asked George, his brow furrowed in concern.

"Nothing definite yet, but it's definitely not a random marking," Jessie mused, her mind racing. "It could be related to this secret society we're investigating."

"Or it might be a red herring meant to throw us off track," countered Bill, his eyes narrowing as he studied the symbol.

"Either way, it's a clue we can't ignore," Jessie insisted. "We need to stay vigilant and keep our eyes open for anything that might be connected to this."

"Agreed," said George, his voice firm. "We'll leave no stone unturned in our quest to uncover the truth."

As they continued their investigation, Jessie felt the pressure mounting. With each step deeper into the shadowy world of covert societies, the stakes grew higher, and the danger loomed ever closer. But she refused to let fear or doubt deter her from her mission.

As the group stood in the dimly lit alleyway, Jessie's thoughts were in turmoil with theories about the mysterious symbol they had just discovered. She turned to her friends and asked, "What do you think? Could this be the mark of the society we're looking into?"

"Perhaps," Bill mused, stroking his chin thoughtfully. "It's definitely unusual, and it was clearly etched for a reason."

"True," George agreed, pacing back and forth. "But we can't jump to conclusions just yet. We should consider all possibilities."

Jessie nodded. "You're right. Let's not lose sight of our goal. We need to keep searching for more clues that could shed light on the connection between these murders and that secret society."

"Speaking of which, there's another crime scene we should investigate," Bill chimed in, pulling out a small notebook from his pocket. "It's an abandoned warehouse in the south end of Liverpool – Aigburth, to be exact. It might hold some answers."

"Let's head there," Jessie suggested, a light burning in her eyes.

The group made their way through the shadowy streets of Liverpool, eventually reaching the deserted warehouse. The moon's faint glow illuminated the crumbling facade of the once-bustling building, casting eerie shadows across its surface. As they pushed open the creaking door, a cold gust of wind rushed past them, sending chills down their spines.

"Creepy place," George muttered under his breath as they stepped inside, pocket torches in hand.

"Perfect for a secret society to conduct its business, wouldn't you say?" Bill remarked, his voice echoing through the vast emptiness of the warehouse.

As their torch beams danced across the walls, Jessie couldn't shake the feeling that something sinister was lurking in the shadows. She found herself scanning every corner, every dark recess, searching for any clue that might help them unravel the mystery at hand.

"Stay sharp, everyone," she warned, her voice hardly above a whisper. "We don't know what we might find here – or who might be watching us."

Inside the warehouse, the eerie silence was almost deafening, broken only by the occasional creak of rotting wooden beams overhead. The faint smell of incense hung in the air, mingling with the musty scent of damp and decay. Jessie's breath caught in her throat as she took in the unsettling atmosphere.

"Can you smell that?" she whispered.

"Smells like incense," George answered, his face scrunching up in distaste. "Why would there be incense in an abandoned warehouse?"

"Only one way to find out," Bill replied, his eyes scanning the darkness.

Khan, still invisible to all except Jessie, twitched his tail to attract Jessie's attention. Jessie watched as Khan's head tilted slightly from side to side as if trying to pinpoint the source of an elusive scent. She knew that Khan had a unique ability to sense supernatural energy – an ability he often downplayed but, in times like these, proved invaluable.

Gesturing to her cat to move away from the group, Jessie asked him, "Khan, what do you make of this place?"

He paused for a moment before answering, his eyes narrowed in concentration. "There's definitely something off about this place, Jessie," he said finally. "It's like... there's a lingering presence of some sort. A residue of supernatural energy."

"Could it be connected to the society we're investigating?" Jessie said, her grip on the torch tightening.

"Maybe," Khan conceded, his gaze sweeping across the vast expanse of the warehouse. "But we'll need more than just a feeling to prove anything. We should keep searching."

As the group continued to explore, Jessie felt a growing unease. The air seemed to grow heavier with every step, and the shadows seemed to close in around them as if hiding secrets just out of reach. Despite the chill in the air, a bead of sweat trickled down her temple. She knew they were on to something – and that knowledge both excited and terrified her.

"Jessie, look!" Bill's voice cut through her thoughts, snapping her back to the present. He was pointing to a wall where the faint remnants of a symbol could be seen, barely visible beneath layers of grime.

"Could it be...?" she trailed off, her heart pounding as the pieces of the puzzle began to fall into place.

"Alright, let's gather our thoughts," Jessie suggested, as they stood in the dimly lit warehouse. She brushed a stray lock of hair behind her ear, her eyes shining with determination. "We have three crime scenes, each with its own eerie atmosphere and strange symbols. What do you chaps make of all this?"

"Almost certainly occult-related," George replied, rubbing his chin thoughtfully. "Those symbols are not something you'd see every day."

"I think so too," Bill chimed in. "But there's more to it than just that. The locations themselves seem to be significant. All three are isolated, hidden away from prying eyes."

"Maybe the secret society uses these places for rituals?" George suggested.

"Could be," Jessie mused. "But we need more concrete evidence if we're going to expose them."

"Then let's move on to the third crime scene," George said, leading the way out of the warehouse. "It's an abandoned church in the heart of Liverpool."

As they approached the church, they couldn't help but feel a sense of desolation washing over them. The once-imposing structure now lay in ruin, its broken stained-glass windows casting eerie, fragmented patterns on the ground. A chilling wind swept through the crumbling archways, carrying with it the faint scent of decay.

Jessie shivered, pulling her coat tighter around her. "This place has seen better days," she murmured, stepping carefully over a pile of rubble.

"Nothing good happens in a place like this," Bill muttered, casting a wary glance at the dark corners of the church.

"Let's focus on finding clues," George urged, nudging aside a fallen beam with his foot. "Keep your eyes peeled for anything unusual."

"Like that?" Bill asked, pointing to a series of cryptic markings etched into the stone wall near the empty altar plinth.

"Exactly," Jessie replied, her voice tinged with excitement. "This could be the break we've been waiting for. Let's not forget our purpose here," Jessie reminded them, her eyes fixed on the symbols. "We owe it to the victims and their families to find the truth behind these murders."

"Absolutely," George agreed, his jaw set in concentration. "We won't rest until we get to the bottom of this."

"Then let's keep moving forward," Jessie said, taking one last look at the abandoned church before leading her friends back out into the night. The mystery was far from solved, but they were one step closer to unravelling the dark secrets hidden within the heart of Liverpool.

"Shh," Jessie whispered, "I think someone from the secret society knows we're here."

"You sure?" Bill asked, his brow furrowed with concern.

"Just a sense of foreboding," Jessie said, unable to tell Bill and George she knew they were being followed because of Khan's supernatural abilities.

"Which means they could know we're onto them," Bill added, his eyes darting around the desolate church, searching for any sign of an unseen watcher. "We need to be careful."

"More than careful," Jessie muttered, "We've got a target on our backs now. We can't let our guard down for even a moment."

"Agreed," Bill said, his voice steely. "Let's get out of here and regroup. We've got a lot of work to do if we're going to build a case against these murderers."

As they slipped out of the unconsecrated grounds of the abandoned church, every rustle of wind through the broken stained-glass windows sent shivers down their spines. They were no longer just investigators; they were now prey in the eyes of the secret organisation. But Jessie's aims never wavered. She knew that they were on the right track, and she would stop at nothing to reveal the truth.

"Stay close," Jessie whispered to her companions as they made their way out into the night, their footsteps echoing softly in the darkness. "We're in this together, and we'll see it through to the end."

With a renewed sense of determination, the group pressed on, stepping out from beneath the shadow of the church and into the unknown dangers that lay ahead.

Margaret

JESSIE DID HER BEST to carry on as normal, but she soon realised the investigation came first. However, she did keep an appointment to entertain her friend Margaret.

Jessie's living room was filled with the sound of laughter, as she and Margaret sat side by side on a plush, floral sofa. A dainty china teapot adorned with pink roses stood regally on the coffee table before them. The sun streamed in through the lace curtains, casting a golden glow over their afternoon tea.

"Jessie, you really must tell me where you found these delightful biscuits," Margaret said between bites. "They're positively scrumptious."

"Ah, it's my own little secret. A small bakery down one of the less-travelled lanes in town." Jessie grinned playfully. "I'll take you there sometime, but I'm afraid if everyone discovers it, they'll be out of stock before I can get my hands on any!"

As the women laughed and chatted, Jessie noticed that Margaret seemed to fidget more than usual, her eyes darting around the room as if looking for something or someone. She thought nothing of it—perhaps Margaret was just having an off day.

Suddenly, Margaret stood up to pour herself another cup of tea. As she reached for the teapot, a folded piece of paper slipped out from her pocket, landing on the floor beside her feet. With her back turned to Jessie, Margaret didn't notice the escaped item.

"Margaret, dear, you dropped something," Jessie remarked, leaning forward to pick up the paper.

Before she could unfold it, Margaret spun around, her eyes wide with momentary panic. "Oh! Thank you, Jessie," she said hastily, attempting to snatch the paper back. But Jessie's curiosity had already been piqued, and she unfolded the paper, revealing a strange symbol drawn on it—a circle with several lines intersecting at odd angles.

"Whatever is this?" Jessie asked, genuinely curious. Margaret's face flushed crimson, and she struggled to come up with an explanation.

"Ah, it's... well, it's nothing important. Just a doodle," she stammered, finally managing to retrieve the paper.

"Curious doodle, though," Jessie mused, her eyes lingering on the symbol before Margaret hastily tucked it away. "I've never seen anything quite like it."

"Really, it's nothing," Margaret insisted, her voice strained. "Just a little something to pass the time, you know?"

Jessie nodded slowly, though her intuition told her that there was more to this strange symbol than her friend was letting on. She decided not to press the matter further—for now. Instead, she sipped her tea and continued their conversation, all the while wondering what secrets Margaret might be keeping. As the sun began to set, casting long shadows across the room, Jessie felt a chill run down her spine. Something was amiss, and she was determined to find out what it was.

"Margaret," Jessie began, her voice gentle yet firm, "that symbol on the paper you dropped... I can't help but feel there's more to it than just a doodle. You've never been one to keep secrets from me before."

Margaret shifted uncomfortably in her seat, her eyes darting away from Jessie's gaze. She fidgeted with the hem of her dress, a clear sign of her unease.

"Jessie, truly, it's nothing important. I don't see why we should dwell on such a trivial matter when there are far more interesting things to discuss."

"Interesting things?" Jessie pressed, raising an eyebrow and leaning forward slightly. "Like what?"

"Like... um, well, have you heard about Mrs Thompson's cat? It's been missing for days!" Margaret blurted out, clearly grasping at straws.

Jessie tilted her head, her gaze unwavering. "I'm more interested in that symbol, Margaret. We've been friends for years, and I know when something is troubling you." She paused, allowing her words to sink in. "Why don't you tell me what's really going on?"

Margaret sighed, running a hand through her hair in frustration. "Jessie, please, let it go. I assure you, it's nothing worth getting worked up over."

Despite Margaret's plea, Jessie couldn't shake the nagging feeling that her friend was hiding something. Her intuition had rarely led her astray, and she wasn't about to disregard it now. She decided to approach the subject from a different angle.

"Alright, Margaret," Jessie conceded, sitting back in her chair and taking a slow sip of her tea. "But if you ever change your mind, I'm here to listen. After all, that's what friends are for, isn't it?"

Margaret looked conflicted, her eyes softening as she met Jessie's gaze. "Yes, that's what friends are for," she agreed quietly, before quickly changing the subject and steering their conversation towards safer topics.

But even as they chatted amiably, Jessie couldn't shake the image of the strange symbol from her mind. She knew Margaret well enough to recognise when something weighed on her conscience, but she also understood the need for patience. Whatever secret lay behind the mysterious mark, she would uncover it in due time. For now, all she could do was wait and watch, trusting her instincts to guide her through this uncharted territory. As the evening wore on and the shadows grew darker, she couldn't help but feel that they were edging ever closer to a hidden truth—one that would test the bounds of their friendship like never before.

Jessie bid Margaret farewell later that evening, watching as her friend disappeared down the dimly lit street. She allowed herself a moment's hesitation, her mind grappling with the decision she was about to make. But curiosity gnawed at her like a persistent itch, and ultimately, it proved too much to ignore.

"Sorry, Margaret, but I have to know," Jessie murmured under her breath, slipping out of her house and following her friend at a cautious distance.

As she trailed Margaret through the darkened streets, Jessie pondered the potential consequences of her actions. If Margaret discovered she was being followed, their friendship could be irreparably damaged. Yet Jessie couldn't shake the feeling that something wasn't right—that Margaret was in danger, or perhaps even involved in something dangerous herself.

The night air was damp and chilly, but Jessie barely noticed the cold as she focused on remaining undetected. Her heart pounded, but she moved with the stealth of a cat, soundlessly navigating the shadowy labyrinth of alleyways and backstreets that made up their bustling city.

Eventually, Margaret stopped outside an old, dilapidated building that Jessie had never paid much attention to before. Glancing around to ensure she wasn't being watched, Margaret slipped inside, disappearing into the darkness within.

Jessie hesitated for only a moment before following suit, her pulse quickening as she stepped into the unknown.

Inside, the room was dim and filled with an eerie, heavy silence. The walls were adorned with mysterious symbols that seemed to dance in the flickering candlelight, casting ominous shadows across the space. Jessie held her breath as she took in the sight before her: a gathering of cloaked figures, their faces hidden beneath deep hoods.

A sudden chill ran down her back, and Jessie pressed herself against the wall, her eyes scanning the room for any sign of Margaret. She felt like an intruder in this secret world, her presence both unwelcome and dangerous. But she couldn't turn back now—not when she was so close to uncovering the truth.

"Brothers and sisters," one of the cloaked figures intoned, their voice low and reverberating throughout the room. "We gather once more to further our cause."

Jessie's heart raced as she listened, her mind filling with questions. Who were these people? What was their purpose? And most importantly, what was Margaret's role in all of this?

As the meeting continued, she strained to catch snippets of conversation, hoping for any piece of information that might shed light on the situation. She heard whispers of clandestine operations and hidden agendas, though the specifics remained frustratingly elusive.

"Enough talk," another figure said, standing up from their seat. "Let us commence the ritual."

The air in the room seemed to thicken with anticipation, and Jessie felt a knot forming in the pit of her stomach. The scene unfolding before her was like something from a nightmare, and she could hardly believe that Margaret—her dear friend Margaret—could be involved in such a sinister gathering.

"Margaret," Jessie thought, her belief wavering, "what have you gotten yourself into?"

Jessie held her breath as she peered around the corner of a dusty bookcase, her eyes riveted on Margaret. Her friend stood among the cloaked figures, her chin raised and hands clasped confidently in front of her. Jessie's heart ached as she watched Margaret nodding along to the proceedings, her betrayal feeling like an icy dagger lodged deep within her chest.

"Margaret," Jessie thought, "how did it come to this?"

"Brother Malachi," Margaret spoke up, her voice steady and commanding, "I have news regarding our latest endeavour."

"Go on, Sister Margaret," Brother Malachi beckoned with a wave of his hand.

The room fell silent, all eyes focused on Margaret as she reported on her activities,— a chilling mix of espionage and manipulation, all carried out under the veil of everyday life. It was clear that Margaret's mission was to discover what Jessie, George and the police knew about the murders. Jessie barely recognised her once-trusted friend, the woman who had shared laughter and tea only hours before.

"Excellent work, Sister Margaret," Brother Malachi praised after she finished speaking. "Your dedication to our cause is commendable."

"Thank you, Brother Malachi," Margaret replied, her face beaming with pride.

"Is this really the same woman I've known for years?" Jessie wondered, her disbelief battling with the cold reality before her. "The one who helped me through my darkest days, who was always there with a comforting word and a friendly smile?"

As the meeting continued, Jessie's resolve hardened. She couldn't stand by and allow this cult or secret society or whatever it was to continue its sinister agenda unopposed. But how could she confront Margaret without losing her dear friend forever?

"Focus, Jessie," she told herself, shaking off her doubts. "Figure out what they're planning, and then deal with Margaret's betrayal later."

"Let us proceed to the initiation of our newest member," Brother Malachi announced, bringing Jessie's attention back to the present.

"Initiation?" Jessie mused, "That sounds... ominous."

As the cloaked figures began to chant in unison, Margaret's eyes locked onto Jessie's hiding place. For a heart-stopping moment, Jessie feared she'd been discovered. But Margaret's gaze shifted away, and Jessie let out a silent sigh of relief.

"Stay hidden, stay focused," Jessie reminded herself, her pulse racing. "Expose the truth and save your friend—no matter the cost."

Jessie's heart pounded as she crouched behind the dusty bookcase, her eyes never leaving Margaret and the cloaked figures. Her thoughts raced, trying to reconcile the image of her dear friend with the woman who now stood among these enigmatic strangers. The betrayal stung like a freshly inflicted wound; Jessie felt as if a part of her very foundation had crumbled away.

"Margaret, how could you?" Jessie whispered under her breath.

She watched as Margaret performed arcane gestures alongside the other initiates, her movements precise and confident. This wasn't a chance encounter or a naive mistake—Margaret was fully committed to this cult.

"Is this really the same Margaret I've known all these years?" Jessie wondered, her mind churning with questions. "The one who'd laugh over tea and gossip about the neighbours? Who shared my love for Agatha Christie novels?"

"Stay focused, Jessie," she scolded herself, shaking her head. "You need to gather evidence, then confront her. If there's any chance of saving Margaret from this darkness, it lies in the truth."

A sudden hush fell over the room, and Jessie's stomach twisted into knots. She realised the gravity of her situation: she was alone, surrounded by enemies, and only a heartbeat away from discovery. She inhaled sharply, drawing upon her reserves of courage.

"Alright then," Jessie muttered, steeling herself. "Time to face the storm."

As the chanting resumed and the initiation ceremony continued, Jessie slipped a small notebook and pen from her pocket. She scribbled down every detail she could: the symbols on the walls, the names spoken aloud, the exact words of their incantations. With each new piece of information, Jessie felt the enormity of her discovery bearing down on her.

"Is this knowledge a blessing or a curse?" she pondered, her hand moving quickly across the page. "Either way, it's a burden I must bear."

"Jessie," Margaret's voice suddenly rang out, and Jessie's heart skipped a beat. She glanced up to see Margaret staring directly at her hiding spot. Time seemed to slow as their eyes locked, and for a moment, Jessie was certain that her friend would expose her presence.

But then, just as quickly, Margaret looked away, her expression unreadable. The initiation continued uninterrupted, leaving Jessie to grapple with a new uncertainty: had Margaret seen her? And if so, what would become of their friendship?

"Only time will tell," Jessie whispered, her eyes fixed on Margaret as she vowed to find the truth behind the secret society and save her friend from its sinister clutches.

Jessie's heart pounded as she continued to observe the society from her hiding spot. She could feel a bead of sweat trickling down her temple, threatening to betray her presence if it reached her trembling hand. Her breaths grew shallow, her fingers tightening around the notebook as she struggled to maintain her composure.

"Stay calm," Jessie whispered to herself, willing her thoughts to quieten. "You've come this far."

"Brothers and sisters," an authoritative voice echoed through the dimly lit room, jolting Jessie back to reality. "The time has come for us to adjourn. Let us seal our pact with the sacred token."

"Here it is," one of the cloaked figures announced, holding up a small, ornate box. The atmosphere in the room shifted, anticipation hanging heavy in the air.

"Margaret?" Jessie questioned in her mind, spotting her friend amongst the gathering. "What on earth possessed you to join this lot?"

Jessie glanced around, frantically searching for an escape route as the cult members began to disperse. She spotted a narrow passageway behind her, but was it too risky?

"Time to make a choice, Jessie," she thought, her instincts screaming at her to flee.

As she cautiously stepped towards the passageway, she froze when she heard footsteps approaching her position. The sound grew louder, reverberating through her very core. Panic surged through her veins, leaving her paralysed with fear.

"Margaret?" a hushed voice called out, stopping just short of Jessie's hiding spot. Jessie held her breath, praying that Margaret would not discover her.

"Over here," Margaret responded, her voice distant. Relief washed over Jessie; her friend hadn't seen her. But the danger was far from over.

"Jessie, you need to get out of here," she urged herself, summoning all her courage to slip away unnoticed. "Your life depends on it."

As Jessie edged towards the passageway, her foot caught on something unexpected - a loose floorboard hidden beneath the shadows. Her heart leapt into her throat as she stumbled forward, barely managing to maintain her balance.

"Almost there," she thought, adrenaline pumping through her veins. The passageway was just within reach when the unthinkable happened: with a soft clatter, her pen fell from her trembling fingers, skittering across the floor and coming to rest at the feet of a cloaked figure. Their eyes met for a split second before the figure's gaze dropped to the incriminating pen.

"Who's there?" the figure demanded, their voice sharp and cold. "Show yourself!"

Jessie's heart hammered, her breaths ragged as she realised there was no escape. She had been discovered, and there was no telling what would happen next.

Jessie's mind raced as the cloaked figure approached. She had to think fast or she may not make it out of this alive. As the figure drew nearer, Jessie noticed a rusted pipe along the wall. It wasn't much, but it could be her only chance.

Just as the figure was about to round the corner, Jessie grabbed the pipe and swung with all her might. A loud crack rang out as metal struck a hard object and the figure crumpled to the ground. Without hesitating, Jessie turned and sprinted down the passageway into the unknown darkness.

The passage twisted and turned, seeming to go on forever. Jessie's lungs burned but she didn't dare slow down. She could hear echoes of shouting behind her as the others discovered what had happened.

Just as Jessie felt she couldn't run any further, the passage opened into a small storeroom. Dusty shelves lined the walls, packed with long-forgotten boxes and supplies. Jessie quickly scanned the room, looking for another way out. In the far corner, a small window hung open, leading out to the gloomy night.

With no time to waste, Jessie scrambled up and through the window. She tumbled out onto damp cobblestones, the chill night air filling her aching lungs. The shouting from the passage was growing louder. Jessie had no choice but to keep running and hope she could make it back home alive.

A Discovery

Jessie slowed to a walking pace after about a mile. She could no longer hear her pursuers.

"You are safe now, Jessie," Khan said.

"Goodness, you startled me," Jessie said. "Where are you? I can't see you."

"Sorry, Jessie, I forgot. I'm here."

Jessie saw Khan right in front of her and he had something in his paw.

"How long have you been with me and what on earth is that you have?" Jessie said.

"Since you entered the meeting room and certainly when Margaret and her cronies discovered you. I made sure you were safe. And this, my dear, is something I swiped from their meeting place."

"How wonderful, you clever cat. Let's get home and see what it is," Jessie said.

Having made it safely home, Jessie leaned over the cluttered table, her hair cascading past her shoulders and forming a curtain around her face as she scrutinised the document that Khan had taken earlier. The dim light from the overhead lamp cast a warm glow on her face, revealing her intense focus on what lay before her.

"Alright," Jessie said, her voice hoarse but steady. "Let's go over what we've found."

"Hmm, *I found*. I swiped this from that meeting place where you saw Margaret," Khan said.

"Sorry, Mr Touchy, I didn't realise I'd hurt your feelings," Jessie said with a smile.

"Facts, Miss Jessie, I'm a facts cat," Khan said.

Ignoring the magical cat, Jessie unfolded the document, her eyes scanning the hastily scribbled notes. A web of names and dates, cryptic symbols, and ominous phrases involving city councillors painted a chilling picture. Jessie knew she must bring the rest of the team in first thing tomorrow.

"Look here," she pointed at a name circled in red ink. "This person must be significant to the secret society. We've seen this name before, haven't we?"

"Right," Khan confirmed, his eyes wide with realisation. "That was one of the murder victims Bill told us about last week."

"Then it's settled," Jessie murmured, "We're closer than ever to uncovering their secrets. But we need to act fast. They now know we're onto them because Margaret saw me at that society meeting and they'll do anything to keep us from the truth."

"I agree," purred Khan. "Jessie," Khan whispered, "There's something else I found."

Khan's paw pointed to a tattered envelope on the table. Jessie tore it open, her eyes widening as she read the cryptic message scrawled in ink:

"Seek the truth beneath the waves."

"Where did you find this?" Jessie asked.

"Hidden behind a loose brick in their meeting place," Khan replied, "I didn't have time to read it before now."

"Neither did they, apparently" Jessie mused, her heart racing as the implications of the message settled in. "We need to figure out what this means. It could be the key to everything."

Jessie tucked the mysterious note into her pocket, and together, she and Khan agreed to update Bill and George the next day.

Dawn came too soon for Jessie following a broken night's sleep but she kept to the plan of updating the rest of the investigative team. They arrived at her flat together at nine precisely that bright morning.

Having told George and Bill about her escape but deliberately omitting Khan's part in the aftermath, all three of the team gathered around the dining table with a shared determination etched on their faces.

"Look at this," Jessie said, her voice low and steady, betraying no hint of the Liverpudlian accent. She pointed to the name circled in red in the document found in the society's lair. "This confirms our suspicions about the society's involvement in the recent string of murders and it also seems it and the council are connected."

George leaned in closer, his dark eyes narrowing as he read the words. "You're right, Jessie. We're definitely onto something here."

"It seems so and a connection to the other murders too," Detective Sergeant Roberts said.

As Jessie continued to piece together the scattered fragments of information, the atmosphere in the room seemed to grow heavier, suffocating her with an intangible sense of dread. She glanced at her colleagues, noticing their growing unease as well.

"Chaps," Jessie began hesitantly, "I can't shake the feeling that they know we're getting closer. I mean, we've been discreet so far, but..."

"Jessie's right," Bill interjected, his voice tinged with anxiety. "Remember the anonymous letter we found pinned to Jessie's flat door last week? 'Beware those who seek the truth.' It's getting too close for comfort."

The silence that followed was deafening, punctuated only by the faint ticking of the wall clock. Everyone exchanged wary looks, acknowledging the importance of their investigation and the danger it posed. Jessie tapped her fingers on the edge of the table, her thoughts hurtling like a race car around the Brooklands track. She knew that each step they took toward uncovering the truth brought them further into the crosshairs of the secret society.

"Alright," Jessie said finally, her voice firm and resolute. "We need to be extra careful from now on. Let's double-check our findings and make sure we're not missing anything that could give them an advantage over us."

"Agreed," Bill replied, his eyes meeting Jessie's with a glint. Together, they delved back into the documents, driven by their pursuit of the truth and the knowledge that they were now playing a dangerous game against a formidable opponent.

A phone ringing broke the silence, jolting Jessie from her focused examination of the documents. Swallowing hard, she answered the call with a cautious "Hello?"

"Listen," the voice on the other end hissed urgently. "They know. They're planning to stop you. Be careful."

"Who is this?" Jessie demanded, but the line went dead. Her hands shook as she lowered the phone, her pulse pounding in her ears.

"Who was that?" Bill asked concern etched on his face.

"A friend, I think, who wishes to stay incognito," Jessie replied, her voice shaky but resolute. "They said the society knows we're close and is planning to stop us."

"Then we have no time to waste," George declared, slamming his fist on the table. "We need to move fast and cover more ground before they can get to us."

Betrayal

A STORM OF EMOTIONS brewed within Jessie as she sat on the edge of her bed, gripping the crumpled document that Khan had found that had just shattered the illusion of trust between her and Margaret. The betrayal stung like a thousand thorns piercing her heart, and she felt shocked, anger, and disappointment all at once. Her mind raced, attempting to make sense of Margaret's involvement in the society. How could someone she considered her closest friend be involved with such a dark organisation? And how could she spy on her?

"Goodness me, Margaret," Jessie muttered under her breath, her hair falling over her face as she shook her head in disbelief. The words on the letter seemed to mock her, taunting her with their revelation. She traced her fingers over the cruel lines of ink, trying to understand why her friend would deceive her like this.

"Think it through, Jessie," she whispered to herself, bent on not letting her emotions cloud her judgment. "You need answers, and you need them now." A fire ignited in her... a fire to confront Margaret and seek the truth.

Jessie stood up abruptly, her tall figure casting a long shadow across the room as the sun began to set outside. With one last glance at the letter, she tucked it into the pocket of her dress - a sleek, high-waisted garment that accentuated her lean frame - and strode out the door.

As Jessie navigated the familiar streets of Liverpool, her thoughts turned to the countless memories she and Margaret had shared over the years. They had laughed, cried, and even bickered together, but they had always been there for each other. And now, with this new revelation hanging over them, their friendship was at stake.

"Where are you, Margaret?" Jessie wondered aloud, narrowing her eyes in determination. She knew she needed to find her friend and have an honest, albeit difficult conversation. There had to be more to the story, some explanation for Margaret's betrayal that Jessie couldn't yet fathom.

"Answers won't come easy," Jessie reminded herself, her lips pursed. "But I won't stop until I understand." With every step, she felt her resolve harden, transforming into a steely armour that would help her face the confrontation that lay ahead.

Jessie's search for Margaret led her through the maze-like streets of Liverpool, her steps echoing in the crisp evening air. She knew it was a long shot, but she held onto the faint hope that she might find her friend at their favourite spot - a secluded garden nestled between a charming row of terraced houses. The garden, with its fragrant flowers and the soothing sounds of a nearby fountain, had always been a haven of solace for the two friends. They had called it their secret garden.

As Jessie approached the entrance to the secret garden, she felt her heart race in anticipation of the confrontation that awaited her. She slipped through the wrought-iron gate, her fingers trembling on the cold metal as she closed it behind her. The fading sunlight cast a melancholy glow over the scene, mirroring the emotional storm brewing within her.

"Margaret," Jessie called out softly, scanning the garden for any sign of her friend. Her voice sounded foreign to her own ears, laced with a vulnerability she rarely allowed herself to reveal.

"Jessie?" came a hesitant reply from behind a cluster of hydrangeas. Margaret emerged slowly, looking both wary and relieved to see her friend. She wore a simple floral dress that contrasted sharply with the complex emotions etched across her face.

"Margaret," Jessie said again, her voice now steady and firm. "I need to know. Did you really join that society? And if so, why?"

"Jessie, I—" Margaret faltered, her eyes darting away from Jessie's piercing gaze. "It's complicated."

"Complicated?" Jessie scoffed, feeling anger swell within her chest like a tidal wave. "You've betrayed our friendship, Margaret! You've been keeping secrets from me, and now I'm left to pick up the pieces!"

"Jessie, please," Margaret pleaded, her eyes welling with tears. "Let me explain."

"Explain?" Jessie snapped, her hair whipping around her face as she shook her head in disbelief. "I trusted you, Margaret. You were my closest friend, and now I find out that you've been involved in some...some secret society? How could you?"

"Jessie," Margaret whispered, her voice cracking with emotion. "I never meant to hurt you. Please, believe me."

"Believe you?" Jessie echoed, her eyes narrowing as she took a step closer to her friend. "How can I trust anything you say anymore, Margaret? Tell me that."

"Jessie, I was desperate," Margaret admitted, her voice barely audible. "I joined the society because I thought it could help me find answers I couldn't find anywhere else. But I never wanted to betray you."

"Answers?" Jessie questioned, her heart pounding as she tried to make sense of Margaret's confession. "What answers could possibly be worth destroying our friendship over?"

"Jessie, I—" Margaret hesitated, biting her lip as she struggled to find the words.

"Tell me, Margaret!" Jessie demanded, her voice shaking with raw emotion. "Or have you become so entangled in this web of deceit that you can't even remember what's real anymore?"

Margaret's eyes brimmed with tears as she stared at Jessie, trying to muster the courage to reveal her darkest secret. "It's about my brother, Thomas," she finally confessed, her voice trembling. "He disappeared five years ago, and I've been searching for him ever since. The police couldn't find any leads, and I was desperate."

"Thomas?" Jessie felt a pang of sympathy mixed with her anger. She remembered Thomas, how he used to tease them when they were younger, before his sudden disappearance. She hadn't known Margaret was still searching for him.

"Jessie, I thought the society could help me find him," Margaret continued, gripping her hands together tightly. "They claimed to have connections and knowledge that went beyond what anyone else could offer. I didn't join them out of malice or greed – I just wanted to find my brother."

As Jessie watched her friend, she could see the pain etched into every line on Margaret's face. She could see the desperation in Margaret's eyes, the same desperation that had driven her to betray their friendship. And despite the hurt Jessie still felt, she couldn't help but empathise with her friend's plight.

"Margaret, I can't believe you never told me about this," Jessie said softly, her anger starting to dissipate as she began to understand Margaret's motivations. "We could have searched together. You didn't have to go through it alone."

"Jessie, I didn't want to burden you," Margaret replied, her voice thick with emotion. "I thought I could handle it on my own. But as time went on, and I found no answers, I grew more and more desperate. That's when the society approached me, promising they could help."

"Did they... did they ever actually help you?" Jessie asked hesitantly, her curiosity piqued despite her lingering resentment.

"Only in small ways," Margaret admitted, shaking her head. "They gave me false leads, vague hints, and empty promises. But I was so desperate that I clung to every shred of hope they offered."

"Margaret, why didn't you leave the society when you realised they weren't helping?" Jessie asked, struggling to comprehend her friend's actions.

"Because they threatened me, Jessie," Margaret whispered, her eyes wide with fear. "They said if I left, they'd make sure I never found Thomas. They made it clear that they had power over me, and I felt trapped."

Jessie's heart ached for her friend, caught between anger at the betrayal and empathy for Margaret's desperation. She knew that forgiving Margaret wouldn't be easy, but she couldn't deny the bond they shared – a bond that went deeper than any secret society could sever.

"Margaret, I don't know if I can ever fully trust you again," Jessie admitted, staring into her friend's tearful eyes. "But I can't turn my back on you, not when you're in this much pain. We'll find Thomas together – without the society's help."

"Jessie, I can't thank you enough," Margaret sobbed, reaching out to grasp Jessie's hand tightly. "For understanding, for giving me another chance."

"Let's just focus on finding Thomas for now," Jessie replied, squeezing Margaret's hand. "We'll figure out the rest as we go."

As they stood there, their fingers entwined and their hearts heavy with emotion, Jessie knew that their friendship would never be the same. Yet, despite the scars left by betrayal and the uncertainty ahead, they were bound by a shared determination to unravel the mysteries that had drawn them apart – and perhaps, in doing so, find a way back to each other.

Margaret's eyes glistened with unshed tears, her voice cracking as she spoke. "Jessie, I am so sorry for everything. I never meant for things to get this far, and I never wanted to hurt you."

Jessie clenched her fists, her knuckles turning white with the effort it took to keep her emotions in check. She stared at the ground, unable to meet Margaret's gaze. The delicate sounds of rustling leaves and distant birdsong did little to soothe her inner turmoil.

"Sorry isn't enough, Margaret," Jessie said softly. "You lied to me, betrayed our trust. How can we ever go back to how things were before?"

"I know I messed up," Margaret admitted, her chin quivering as she fought to hold back her sobs. "I just... I was so lost, Jessie. I thought I could find some answers, some sense of purpose within the society. But I see now that all I've done is destroy our friendship."

"Actions have consequences, Margaret." Jessie's words were heavy with pain, her heart feeling as if it were being squeezed into a vice. "Can I really forgive you for what you've done? Can we ever truly be friends again?"

Margaret's shoulders sagged, and she looked utterly defeated. "I understand if you can't forgive me, Jessie. But please know that I am truly, deeply sorry. And no matter what happens, I will always cherish the friendship we had."

Jessie sighed, her chest tightening as she struggled to contain the tempest of emotions swirling within her. Anger and hurt warred with empathy and an instinctive desire to protect her friend from further harm. It was a harrowing decision, one that threatened to tear her apart from the inside out.

"Margaret..." Jessie hesitated, her thoughts racing like a storm-tossed sea. "I can't pretend that things will ever be the same between us. And I don't know if I can ever fully trust you again. But... I'm willing to try. To rebuild our friendship, slowly and cautiously, if you're willing to do the same."

The relief that flooded Margaret's face was palpable, and Jessie could see the weight lifting from her friend's shoulders as she nodded vigorously. "Yes, Jessie, I am more than willing. Thank you for giving me a chance to make things right."

"Let's take it one step at a time," Jessie cautioned, feeling a small flicker of hope amidst the ruins of their shattered friendship. "And remember Margaret – no more secrets. From now on, we face whatever comes our way together."

As they stood in the secluded spot, Jessie knew that their path forward would not be an easy one. But with honesty and perseverance, perhaps they could find a way to heal the wounds inflicted by betrayal and restore the bond that had once been so strong.

The atmosphere between Jessie and Margaret was as taut as a wire pulled to its breaking point, their stances mirroring the tension that crackled in the air. As they stood in the secluded glade, fading shafts of sunlight pierced through the canopy of leaves overhead, casting an ethereal glow on the scene, a stark contrast to the storm of emotions brewing within them.

"Jessie," Margaret implored once more, her voice a tremulous whisper, "I know I've hurt you deeply, but I swear to you, it was not my intention. Please, give me a chance to prove myself."

Jessie's gaze never wavered from Margaret's pleading eyes, her own heart a cacophony of conflicting sentiments. She felt the sting of betrayal like a slap to the face, and yet, the memory of years of laughter and shared secrets tugged at her heartstrings, refusing to be silenced.

"Margaret," Jessie said, her tone measured, though her thoughts whirled like fallen leaves caught in a gust of wind, "our friendship has been a beacon in my life, our bond something I've cherished beyond measure. But this... this deception cuts deeper than any wound I've ever known."

The anguish in Jessie's voice was palpable, her words an echo of the tempest raging within her soul. Memories of their long walks along the waterfront, late-night conversations over cups of tea, and countless moments of shared joy and sorrow danced before her mind's eye, a bittersweet reminder of what once was.

"Forgiving you means opening myself up to the possibility of being hurt again," Jessie continued, her voice wavering with the burden of her internal struggle. "And I don't know if I have the strength to do that."

"Jessie," Margaret pleaded, desperation seeping into her every word, "I understand your fear, your anger. But I promise you, from the depths of my heart, that I will do everything in my power to regain your trust and prove that our friendship is worth fighting for."

Margaret's sincerity was unmistakable, her remorse evident in the tremble of her voice and the tears glistening in her eyes. And as Jessie stood there, torn between the shadows of betrayal and the light of forgiveness, she knew that the decision before her would change the course of their lives forever.

"Margaret," Jessie said, at last, her voice heavy, "I cannot make any promises. But I am willing to try... to see if we can find our way back to each other."

The tiny spark of hope that ignited within Margaret's eyes spoke volumes, and Jessie could feel the first tentative threads of reconciliation weaving their way between them, fragile yet alive.

"Thank you, Jessie," Margaret whispered, her gratitude shining through her tears.

As they walked away from the glade, side by side but worlds apart, Jessie knew that the road ahead would be fraught with obstacles and moments of doubt. But with honesty and perseverance, perhaps they could find a way to rekindle the flame of friendship that had once burned so bright.

The air was thick with tension as Jessie stood there, caught in a whirlwind of thoughts and emotions. Margaret's face was pale, her eyes wide with fear and hope - a mirror reflecting Jessie's own uncertainty.

"Let's start anew," Jessie said softly, her gaze fixed on the darkening sky. "We can't change the past, but we have the power to shape our future."

"Agreed," Margaret replied, a newfound hope in her voice.

The lingering shadows of doubt and betrayal began to recede as they moved forward, leaving behind the first seeds of hope and forgiveness. And with each step they took, the once-fragile threads of their friendship began to grow stronger, intertwining and weaving a new tapestry that was both familiar and uncharted.

Thus, the chapter closed on the painful revelations and raw emotions of the day. But there were many more pages yet to be written, their ink waiting to trace the journey of two friends learning to trust anew and redefine the ties that bound them.

Hostage

The phone rang, its shrill tone shattering Jessie's concentration as she sat in her living room, poring over the notes of her investigation. The darkness outside framed the window like a sinister shadow, and the wind whistled eerily through the trees.

"Hello?" Jessie answered, her hair falling softly over her face as she held the receiver to her ear.

"Miss Jessie, we have George," a guttural voice spat from the other end of the line, causing her heart to drop.

"Who is this? What do you want with him?" Jessie demanded, her Liverpool upbringing seeping into her voice as she fought to control the panic rising within her.

"Your meddling stops now. If you continue your investigation, George will suffer the consequences," the voice warned before hanging up abruptly.

"No!" Jessie slammed the phone down, her hands shaking with fear and fury. She had no time to waste; she needed to find George and dismantle this secret society once and for all.

Khan, her enigmatic companion gifted with supernatural abilities, appeared silently at her side. He sensed her panic, his piercing green eyes searching her face for answers. "Jessie, what happened?" he asked, his voice a calming balm amidst the chaos.

"George has been kidnapped by this secret society I've been investigating. They're threatening to hurt him if I don't back off." Jessie's hands clenched into fists, her nails digging into her palms. "I can't just abandon him, Khan."

"Of course not, Jessie. We have a mission to complete, and rescuing George is now part of it. We'll find him and bring him back safely." Khan moved closer, placing a reassuring paw on her shoulder. "But you must stay focused. Do not let your emotions cloud your judgment."

Jessie took a deep breath, steadying herself. "You're right, Khan. I need to keep a clear head if we're going to save George and bring this society down."

"Exactly," Khan nodded, his gaze never leaving hers. "We have resources, skills, and determination on our side. We will succeed, Jessie. Just trust in yourself and in our mission."

Knowing she must find George, Jessie dialled the familiar number of her trusted friend and ally, Detective

Sergeant Bill Roberts. The line buzzed and crackled, mimicking the whirlwind of emotions churning within her.

"Bill, it's Jessie," she said urgently once he picked up. "George has been kidnapped by that secret society we've been investigating. I need your help."

"Kidnapped?" Bill's voice was tinged with disbelief and concern. "Good grief, Jessie, are you alright?"

"Never mind me. I'm worried about George," Jessie replied, pacing back and forth, her worn shoes squeaking against the wooden floor. She could feel Khan's watchful gaze on her as she spoke, his presence a comforting anchor in an increasingly turbulent sea. "I'm hoping you can help us locate their lair."

"Alright, let me think..." Bill muttered, the sound of rustling papers filtering through the phone line. "You know, I've heard rumours about a hidden underground network that the secret society operates from. Tunnels and passageways hidden beneath the city."

"Underground network?" Jessie's heartbeat quickened, her hair dancing around her face as she looked expectantly at Khan. "How do we find it?"

"From what I gather, there's an entrance near the new Queensway Tunnel. It's well-guarded, though, so you'll need to be cautious." Bill's voice became more serious, his concern for his friends evident. "Please, Jessie, be careful. And keep me updated."

"Thank you, Bill. We'll bring George back safely, I promise," Jessie vowed, her grip tightening around the phone. As she disconnected the call, she turned to Khan, "We have a lead. Let's go."

Khan nodded, his piercing eyes reflecting the fire burning within Jessie. "Together, we'll save George and bring down this cult."

With each step towards the new Queensway Tunnel, Jessie's thoughts were a whirlwind of strategy and concern for George. She knew she had to trust in her abilities and her allies, but her heart couldn't help but flutter with fear. The mission was a big responsibility yet her will power remained steadfast as they ventured into the unknown.

Jessie could almost feel the dampness of the underground network as she and Khan huddled together in an unused watchman's hut a few hundred yards from the new road tunnel entrance. Using Jessie's pocket torch, they were looking at a makeshift map, plotting their infiltration. The tiny room felt like a sanctuary in this dangerous world they found themselves in. Luckily, Khan had made himself invisible when Jessie heard a familiar Welsh voice.

"Right you are, young lady, I knew I would probably find you here." Detective Sergeant Bill Roberts said.

"Am I glad to see you, Bill. I knew you would rescue George. After all, you saved his life in the trenches so I'm sure you going to protect him from this cult," Jessie said.

"That's right," Bill said.

"Alright," Jessie said, tapping her sharp nails on the map, her hazel eyes narrowing at the crisscrossing lines that represented the secret society's lair. "According to your intel, Bill, there are three main entrances, all guarded by the society's members. Is that right?"

"Correct." Bill nodded, "but I also believe this is a less known entrance here—" as he pointed to a small dot on the map "—that might be our best bet."

"Fewer people means fewer chances of being caught," Jessie agreed, her lips pursed in contemplation. "What about their security measures?" Bill said.

"Probably some occult stuff we don't know about," Jessie mused, her hair falling over her shoulder as she leaned closer to the map. She could feel the gentle tickle of anxiety in her chest but pushed it away, focusing on the task at hand.

"Then we'll need disguises," Bill suggested, running a hand through his hair. "Something that will help us blend in with their members."

"Good idea," Jessie said, her mind already racing with possibilities. "We'll also need lock-picking tools for George's restraints and any doors we encounter."

"Leave that to me," Khan said telepathically so only Jessie could hear, "I've got a few tricks up my sleeve."

"Perfect." Jessie said for Khan's ear only and then added for Bill's benefit, "I think we can deal with all that if and when we encounter such things." She glanced between her two allies, feeling a surge of gratitude for their unwavering support. "Now let's gather what we need and get moving. We don't have much time."

Jessie and Bill set to work, scouring their surroundings for anything that could aid in their mission. Jessie found an old trunk filled with dusty clothes—perfect for disguises—and began sorting through them, her fingers brushing against worn fabric. She could feel history in each garment, and it only strengthened her resolve.

"Here," she said, tossing one of two long, dark cloaks to Bill. "These should help us blend in."

"Good find." Bill caught his cloak with ease, draping it over his broad shoulders. The material seemed to take on a life of its own, shifting colours to match his outfit perfectly.

"Now we just need to make sure our faces aren't recognisable," Jessie said.

"Leave that to me," Bill chimed in, rummaging through a bag he had brought along. He pulled out small containers of makeup and prosthetics, the tools of a master of disguise. "We'll be unrecognisable in no time."

As Bill finished his task transforming their appearances, Jessie focused on gathering other necessary items that could be used as weapons to defend themselves. Everything felt surreal, like a scene from one of those old detective novels she used to read as a child.

"Alright," Jessie breathed, her heart pounding as she looked at her disguised companion. "Let's go save George."

With their disguises in place, Jessie, Bill and the invisible magical cat, Khan, set off into the night, ready to face the unknown and bring their friend back home.

THE TRIO VENTURED INTO the shadows, their footsteps muffled by the cloak of darkness that had enveloped them. Jessie led the way, her auburn hair tucked beneath a hood that made her eyes gleam like embers in the night. Khan and Bill followed close behind, Bill's face obscured by makeup and prosthetics and Khan invisible to all and sundry.

"Jessie, remember the map," Khan whispered telepathically. "We need to look for the hidden entrance."

"Aye, I've got it right here," she said but only Khan could hear. She fished out the map from her pocket and unfolded it carefully. As she studied the intricate lines and symbols, an eerie feeling settled over Jessie. She knew there must be a supernatural element to all this; no ordinary secret society could have remained hidden for so long.

"Alright, we're here," Jessie announced, pointing to a nondescript alleyway with a small, barely visible door. "This is where the hidden passages begin. Let's go."

As they entered the winding network of tunnels, the atmosphere grew heavier, the air thick with the scent of damp earth and something else, something sinister. Jessie couldn't quite put her finger on it, but she knew they were not alone.

"Bill, can you sense anything?" she asked, her voice betraying a hint of trepidation.

"Nothing specific, but there's definitely something here," he replied, his eyes scanning the darkness. "Stay alert."

They moved cautiously through the intricate passageways, each step echoing ominously as they tried to avoid detection. At one point, Jessie felt that familiar sudden chill run down her spine as though someone – or something – was watching them.

"Did you feel that?" she whispered, her heart racing.

"Feel what?" Bill asked, his brow furrowed in confusion.

"Never mind," Jessie replied, shaking off the sensation. "Let's keep moving."

As they approached the inner sanctum, the traps and obstacles became more treacherous. A tripwire lay hidden in the shadows, waiting to ensnare an unwary foot. Jessie spotted it just in time, her keen senses attuned to the supernatural.

"Watch your step," she warned, pointing out the almost invisible wire. With careful steps, they continued forward, only to encounter a door that seemed impossibly locked.

"Jessie, this is where your lock-picking skills come in handy," Bill said, his eyes fixed on the daunting mechanism.

"Right," she muttered under her breath, "little does Bill know this is where Khan earns his keep."

Khan still disguised in his cloak of invisibility performed his magic over the lock whilst Jessie feigned movements so it looked like her fingers were deftly manoeuvring something to unlock the door.

"Got it!" Jessie exclaimed triumphantly, the lock clicking open as if she had picked the lock. They pushed through the door and into the lair, their hearts pounding with anticipation.

"Stay close," Bill instructed, his voice low and steady. "We're almost there."

The dark corridor stretched out before them, illuminated by the flickering wall torchlights casting eerie shadows on the rough stone walls. Jessie's heart pounded as she took a cautious step forward, feeling the cold dampness beneath her feet. She could sense that they were close to finding George but knew that any misstep could lead to disaster.

"Wait," Bill said, "someone or something is nearby."

Jessie and Bill exchanged anxious glances, their breaths catching in their throats.

"Can you tell which way they're coming from?" Jessie whispered, her fingers tightening around the stick she had gathered as a weapon.

Bill closed his eyes for a moment, his brow furrowing with concentration. "Footsteps like someone patrolling further down the corridor, moving away from us for now. But we must be swift and silent."

"Right," Jessie murmured, her resolve strengthening. This was no time for hesitation; George was depending on them. "Bill, I'll stay close to you."

The still invisible feline, Khan, unknown to Bill and Jessie was leading the way and using a magical force field was towing the two humans in his wake. However, Jessie sensed Khan was using his supernatural abilities to lead them to George.

In that knowledge and as they crept along the shadowy passageway, Jessie admired Khan's uncanny ability to navigate the treacherous terrain. It was as if he was attuned to some unseen frequency, guiding them safely through the hidden dangers lurking around every corner.

At last, they reached a heavy wooden door, its iron hinges groaning softly as Bill pushed it open just enough to peer inside. His face paled, and Jessie felt her stomach clench with dread.

"George is in there," Bill whispered, his voice strained. "He's tied to a chair but seems unharmed... for now. Let's get him out of here," Bill said grimly, his eyes meeting Jessie's in a look of steely determination.

"Agreed," Jessie replied, taking a deep breath to steady her nerves. "But we need to be careful not to alert the guards."

Jessie knew Khan would keep watch whilst Bill and she went into the room.

Jessie and Bill slipped inside, their hearts hammering as they approached George. He looked up at them with a mixture of relief and terror, his eyes pleading for help.

"Thank heavens you found me," George whispered hoarsely, struggling against his bonds. "These people are mad!"

"Shh, we're going to get you out of here," Jessie reassured him, her fingers flying deftly over the knots that held him captive. "Just stay calm and try not to make any noise."

As the last knot came undone, George slumped forward, his body trembling with exhaustion and fear. But there was no time to console him – they had to get out before the guards discovered George's absence.

"Come on, we have to move," Bill urged, his arm wrapped around George for support.

"Stay close, and stay quiet," Jessie whispered as they retraced their steps, their escape now more urgent than ever. She couldn't help but wonder what awaited them next, and how far the society would go to protect their dark secrets. But one thing was certain: they had to save George and bring the society down.

Jessie's heart raced, and her mind churned with thoughts of what could go wrong. What if they ran into more guards? What if George couldn't keep up? She shook her head, banishing the negative thoughts. They had come this far, and she would not let her fears stand in the way of rescuing her friend.

Once more the invisible Khan led the way. "Almost there," Khan whispered telepathically so only Jessie could hear. They approached the passage that would lead them to freedom. "Just a bit further," Khan said again.

But as they rounded the corner, a chilling voice echoed through the corridor, stopping them in their tracks. "Going somewhere?"

Otherworldly Power

The voice was that of a leader. It spoke with authority.

Jessie's blood ran cold as the secret society's leader stepped out from the shadows, his eyes glowing with otherworldly power. The air crackled with malevolence, and Jessie knew they were in grave danger.

"Release him immediately," the leader demanded, his voice dripping with menace as he gestured towards George. "You have no idea what you're meddling with."

"Never!" Jessie spat back, her fierce resistance rising to meet the occasion. "We won't let you use him for your twisted rituals."

"Very well." The leader raised his hands, sending a wave of dark energy hurtling towards them. "Then you shall all perish together."

Khan's disembodied voice rang out, "Run!" Only Jessie could see he had lunged forward to shield Jessie and the others from the incoming force. As the impact rippled through the corridor, Jessie knew there was no turning back – they had to escape or die trying.

Oblivious to Khan's efforts, Bill shouted, "Keep moving!" His voice strained with effort as he helped support George. "We can't let him stop us!"

Jessie nodded. They had come too far to give up now. With Khan, she would face whatever dangers lay ahead and bring George home safely. And, perhaps most importantly, they would finally expose this cult and put an end to its reign of terror once and for all.

As the dark energy surged towards them, Jessie's heart raced, and she knew they had little time to react. Still in his cloak of invisibility, Khan sprang into action, his supernatural abilities allowing him to deflect some of the force, while Bill charged at their assailants with a ferocity that belied his age.

"Jessie, we need a plan!" Bill yelled over the din of battle, his eyes still glowing with determination.

"Right!" Her mind raced as she assessed the situation. "Keep them busy! I will find something to use against them!"

"Got it!" Bill replied, his muscles tense as he scanned the room for any potential weapons.

Jessie's gaze fell upon an ancient-looking ceremonial dagger on a nearby dais, its blade gleaming wickedly in the dim light. She snatched it up, praying it would be enough to turn the tide in their favour.

"Here goes nothing," she muttered under her breath, grasping the dagger firmly in her hand.

Jessie was the only one to hear Khan. "Jessie, watch out!" He shouted. She turned just in time to dodge a blast of energy from one of the cult's followers. The air around her crackled with electricity, making the hairs on the back of her neck stand on end.

"Nice try!" Jessie taunted, her adrenaline-fuelled courage carrying her forward. She lunged toward the attacker, the dagger raised high above her head.

"Bill, now!" Jessie roared, her eyes locked on the leader.

With a grunt of effort, Bill hurled a heavy candlestick at the leader's head, momentarily stunning him. Jessie seized the opportunity, pouncing on the man and pinning him to the ground.

"Jessie, finish this!" Bill urged as she struggled to keep the man immobilised.

Her heart pounding, Jessie knelt over the leader, the ceremonial dagger at the ready. She hesitated for a moment owing to doubt and fear. What if this wasn't enough to stop him? What if she failed? What if she could not kill?

Then a voice only she could hear: "Jessie, you can do this, you must do it!" Khan reassured her, his voice strained but steady. "We believe in you."

With one last deep breath, Jessie drove the dagger into the leader's chest, praying it would be enough to end his reign of terror.

As the blade pierced his flesh, the leader let out an anguished scream, the air around him pulsing with dark energy. His body convulsed, then went limp beneath Jessie's grasp, before turning into dust. The secret society's followers fled in terror, their once-unshakeable loyalty shattered by the sight of their fallen leader.

"Is... is it over?" Jessie panted, her entire body trembling from the exertion.

"Looks like it," Khan said, "you did it, Jessie."

"Khan, shush, what if anyone hears you?" Jessie said.

"It's alright, Bill got knocked unconscious in the melee. He is okay but can't hear me and George may as well be unconscious too..."

"Oh my, why?"

"Those blasts of energy summoned up by the leader and his followers have rendered George into a temporary state of disorientation. He can't see or hear a thing."

"Oh, poor George," Jessie said.

"Yes, but we survived," Khan said.

"Only because we did it together," she said, looking between Khan and Bill with gratitude shining in her eyes. "Now, let's get George out of here and finish what we started."

"George, are you alright?" Jessie asked, her voice laced with concern as she gently checked his wrists for abrasions from the restraints.

"Been better, but I'll manage," he replied, rubbing his wrists to restore circulation. "Thanks to you and Bill."

"Let's get out of here," Jessie said, her eyes scanning the dim room for any hidden dangers.

Now recovered, Bill said, "Agreed," and in his mind he was already retracing their steps.

They carefully navigated the hidden passages, their senses heightened and muscles tense. The air was thick with dust and shadows, casting an eerie atmosphere over their escape. Every sound – the echoing drip of water, the distant scuttle of a rat – made them pause, prepared for the worst.

"Jessie, you were amazing back there," George whispered as they cautiously moved through the underground labyrinth. "I don't think I've ever seen anyone so brave."

"Bravery isn't about not being scared, George," Jessie replied, her voice wavering slightly. "It's about pushing through the fear to do what needs to be done."

"Still," George insisted, shooting her a grateful smile, "we wouldn't have made it without you."

Jessie returned the smile, feeling the burden of responsibility she bore for her friends' safety. As they continued their way out, she felt the comforting presence of Khan, his reassuring energy bolstering her courage.

As they neared the exit, the stale air gave way to a faint, fresh breeze. The scent of damp earth and moss filled their nostrils, signalling that freedom was close at hand. A collective sigh of relief escaped their lips as they finally emerged into the moonlit night, the hideout receding into the darkness behind them.

"Never been so glad to see the sky," Bill remarked, a rare sentimentality in his tone.

"Me neither," Jessie agreed, her heart swelling with relief at their success.

"Jessie," Bill said, his eyes meeting hers with a fierce intensity, "we did it. We saved George, and now we can continue our pursuit of the truth."

"Thanks to all of you," she replied, feeling her sense of purpose surge anew. "Now let's put an end to this cult once and for all."

As they stood beneath the starry expanse, united by their shared purpose and camaraderie, Jessie knew that nothing could stand in their way. Together, they would face whatever obstacles lay ahead – and emerge victorious.

Jessie led the group to a safe distance from the underground lair, carefully choosing a spot concealed by an ancient oak tree. The moonlight filtered through the leaves as they settled down on the damp earth.

"Let's go over everything," Jessie began, recalling the details of their harrowing experience. "We need to make sure we have all the information necessary to bring this secret society to justice."

"Right," George chimed in, rubbing his wrists where the restraints had been. "I overheard a few things while I was captive." He recounted what he had learned about the society's plans and key members, his words tinged with anger.

"Any specifics, George?" Jessie said.

"Councillor Thompson is a member and he's involved in some fraud over building permits. Let me think... yes, those murder victims were killed by the society to keep them quiet." George said.

"Good work, George," Bill said. "With that information, we can start dismantling their operation."

"Agreed," George said, his voice steady and resolute. "But we'll need a plan. They won't go down without a fight."

As Jessie listened to the others, she stared at the ground, her hair falling across her face like a curtain. She knew there was no room for error in their next move. Her friends' lives were at stake, and she couldn't afford to let them down.

"Okay," Jessie said, inhaling and looking up at her companions. "Here's what we're going to do." She outlined a meticulous plan, drawing upon her knowledge of the supernatural and the unique skills of her team.

"Are you sure about this?" George asked hesitantly, sensing the inherent risks involved.

"Dead sure," Jessie replied firmly, her eyes blazing with conviction. "It's the only way to stop them - and keep everyone safe."

"Jessie's right," Bill agreed, placing a hand on her shoulder. "Together, we can overcome anything."

"Alright then," George said with a nod, his face set in determination. "Let's put an end to this nightmare."

As the group moved away from their meeting place, Jessie felt a sense of purpose welling up inside her, a fierce resolve that would see them through the difficult and dangerous times ahead.

"Let's do this," she whispered, hardly heard above the rustling leaves and nocturnal creatures. "Together."

And with that, they disappeared into the night, each step bringing them closer to their ultimate showdown with the secret society - and the final reckoning that awaited them all.

Who Did I Kill?

ONE WEEK LATER

Jessie met George and Bill in the Kardomah café after Bill had requested the meeting. Over coffees, Bill showed them a typewritten note that had been delivered anonymously to Hatton Garden police station addressed to Jessie Harper c/o Detective Sergeant Bill Roberts.

In bold typescript, it bore the message:

YOU BELIEVE YOU KILLED ME BUT YOU DIDN'T. MEET ME AT THE ABANDONED WAREHOUSE ON CAZNEAU STREET. 10 PM FRIDAY. COME ALONE. I PROMISE YOU WILL NOT BE HURT.

"Well, if I didn't kill the leader, who did I kill?" Jessie said.

"And… who wrote this letter?" George said,

"There's only one way to find out," Bill said.

Unseen and unheard by anyone other than Jessie, Khan whispered, "Go. I will protect you. Trust me."

"Yes, I go alone," Jessie said.

"What!" George said.

"Preposterous!" Bill exclaimed.

"I'll brook no dissent," Jessie said and two grown men knew it was best not to argue.

JESSIE'S INSTINCTS WERE PRICKLING like a thousand tiny needles, warning her that something was amiss. Despite the usual 1930s traffic noises and the usual cacophony of sounds from the Liverpool streets even at ten in the evening, an eerie stillness seemed to hang in the air as she approached the dimly lit, abandoned warehouse in Cazneau Street close to the dock road, the main arterial road following the coast north to Seaforth then beyond to Preston.

Jessie saw Khan's green eyes glowing through his cloak of invisibility. The faithful feline said nothing. He simply gave a reassuring nod.

"Of all the places for a meeting," she muttered to herself, trying to keep her voice steady. The secret society's leader had chosen this location to confront Jessie, and it was clear that subtlety was not his forte. Was it the leader though? If she didn't kill the leader, who did she kill?

The warehouse towered above her, its empty windows shadowed by grime and neglect. Crows perched along the corroded rafters, their beady eyes following Jessie's every movement. The wind whistled through the cracks in the building, sending a shiver down her back.

"Get a grip, Jessie," she whispered under her breath, steeling herself for the confrontation that awaited her inside.

As Jessie stepped into the cavernous interior of the warehouse, the darkness seemed to swallow her whole. Her eyes scanned the gloom, searching for any sign of life. A faint, flickering light near the centre of the room finally caught her attention.

"Good of you to join us, Miss Jessie," came a deep, sinister voice from the shadows. A man emerged, his tall figure bathed in the weak glow from a single, swaying bulb hanging above him. He looked menacing, with an air of command that left no doubt as to who was in control here.

"Who are you?" Jessie demanded, attempting to mask the fear that threatened to rise in her throat. "What do you want with me?"

"Ah, the feisty spirit we've heard so much about," he replied, a cruel smile playing on his lips. "You've been poking your nose into our affairs, Miss Jessie, and I must say, your curiosity is both impressive and... inconvenient."

"I assume you are the Hawk, the leader of this organisation, and your lot have been causing trouble around here for far too long," Jessie shot back, her eyes narrowing in defiance. "We know you and your lot are connected to the murders and somehow to the council. It's about time someone put a stop to it."

"Really?" he asked, raising an eyebrow. "And you think you're the one to do it?"

"Someone has to be," she replied, her voice strained with a fear of the unknown.

The leader chuckled darkly, clearly enjoying this game of cat and mouse. "Well, I must warn you, Miss Jessie, that you are meddling with forces beyond your comprehension. We have knowledge and power that you cannot possibly fathom."

"Is that supposed to scare me?" Jessie retorted, trying to sound braver than she felt.

"Only a fool wouldn't be scared," he said, his voice ice-cold. "But by all means, continue down this path, if you wish. Just remember, there will be consequences."

"Are you threatening me?" Jessie asked, her heart pounding.

"Merely stating a fact," he replied, his tone dripping with menace. "You've been warned, Miss Jessie. Interfere with us again, and you'll find out just how powerful we truly are."

"Are you going to kill me?" Jessie blurted out, trying to steel herself for whatever answer might come.

"Kill you?" The leader echoed her words with an unnerving smile. "No, my dear, death would be far too kind."

Jessie's mind raced, trying to decipher his cryptic words and what they might mean to her. She needed more information, something that might help her escape his clutches and perhaps even bring down the society itself.

"Then what is it that you want from me?" she asked, as bravely as she could manage.

"Ah, always so curious." The leader seemed amused by her defiance. "You'll find out soon enough. But for now, know that you've stumbled into a world far beyond your comprehension. You cannot possibly fathom the forces at play here."

"And what if I refuse to submit to your... plans?" Jessie questioned, her voice shaking despite her best efforts.

"Refuse?" The leader tilted his head, considering her words. "Your defiance is admirable but ultimately futile. You will come to understand, in time. We all have our roles to play, Miss Jessie. Yours has just begun."

His words hung heavy in the air, leaving Jessie with a sense of impending doom. She knew she was outmatched and in grave danger, but she couldn't – wouldn't – give up without a fight. As the leader's cryptic threats echoed through the warehouse, Jessie braced herself for whatever horrors lay ahead.

Jessie swallowed hard, feeling the cold damp air of the warehouse pressing down on her. She couldn't afford to show fear, not now. She had to find out more about this group and its intentions.

"Your threats don't scare me," Jessie managed to say, trying to maintain an air of confidence. "I've faced more dangerous things than you."

"Have you now?" The leader's voice oozed with menace as he raised his hands, palms facing up. Before her eyes, a small flame appeared, suspended in mid-air above one hand, while a tiny whirlwind formed above the other. Jessie's heart raced, but she refused to let her astonishment show.

"Child's play," she scoffed, even though her mind screamed otherwise. "I've seen street performers do better."

"Ah, but they are mere illusionists." The leader's eyes gleamed with malice as the flames and wind swirled together, forming a pulsing orb of flickering light and shadows. "This is real power, Miss Jessie. Power that can be harnessed... or used as a weapon."

"Is this how your precious society maintains control?" Jessie asked, unable to tear her gaze away from the mesmerising display. "By terrorising people with parlour tricks?"

"Parlour tricks?" The leader laughed, a sound that sent shivers down Jessie's spine. "You still see nothing, do you? This world is filled with secrets, hidden truths, and forces beyond mortal understanding. And we, the members of this society, hold the keys to unlocking them."

"Then what do you want with me? I'm just an ordinary woman."

"Ordinary?" The leader smirked, allowing the orb to dissipate into wisps of smoke. "Hardly. You possess a tenacity, a determination, that few others can boast. It has led you here, to us, and it is that very character trait that will seal your fate."

"Is that a threat?" Jessie's voice wavered, but she clenched her fists at her sides, trying to project an air of defiance.

"Consider it... a warning. You have stumbled into a world you cannot escape." The leader glanced around the warehouse, his gaze finally settling back on her. "You can either join us, learn our secrets, and become part of something greater than yourself... or face the consequences of your meddling."

Jessie's mind raced, torn between her desire for answers and her fear of the unknown. She couldn't give in to this man, this society, but the thought of facing whatever arcane forces they controlled made her blood run cold. Still, she knew she had to find a way out – for herself, and for others who might be caught in their web.

"Fine," she said, forcing the word out through gritted teeth. "I'll play your game. But don't think for a moment that I'll be one of your pawns."

"Time will tell, Miss Jessie," the leader replied, his eyes narrowing as he regarded her with a mix of curiosity and wariness. "Time will tell."

The leader's footsteps echoed in the cavernous warehouse as he began to circle Jessie, his eyes never leaving hers. Each step felt like a tightening vice around her chest, forcing her to confront the gravity of the situation she now found herself in.

"Tell me, Miss Jessie," he said, his voice low and menacing, "why do you think you can take on forces that have existed for centuries? You, a woman who barely understands the world she has stumbled into."

Jessie took a deep breath, struggling to maintain her composure. She couldn't let him see how much he unnerved her. "I don't know what I'm up against, it's true. But I've learned enough to know that whatever you're doing, it isn't right. And I won't stand by whilst innocent people are hurt."

"Ah, yes," the leader sneered, continuing his slow orbit around her. "The righteous heroine, fighting for the truth about the murders and the death of her friend, Elsie. How noble of you." He paused, tilting his head as he scrutinised her. "But nobility won't protect you from the darkness you're meddling with."

Jessie clenched her jaw, trying to block out the cold tendrils of fear that threatened to overtake her. She had to remember why she was here – to discover the truth about this outfit and put an end to its sinister machinations. But as she stood there, surrounded by shadows and faced with the leader's taunts, she couldn't help but feel a creeping sense of despair.

What if she wasn't strong enough? What if she couldn't save anyone from the danger this society posed?

"Your fear is evident, Miss Jessie," the leader remarked casually, pausing directly behind her. "But you must understand one thing" – he leaned in close, his breath hot against her neck –"our power is absolute. Your attempts to resist us are futile. You will either join us or be consumed by the very darkness you seek to destroy."

"Never," Jessie whispered, "I won't let you win."

"Brave words," the leader said, his voice dripping with disdain as he straightened up and resumed his circling. "But bravery alone won't save you. In fact... " – he grinned cruelly –"it may just hasten your downfall."

Jessie's heart hammered as she realised the magnitude of the threat she faced. The leader was a formidable adversary, one who wielded power beyond her wildest imaginings. But she couldn't back down now – too much was at stake.

And so, despite the terror that clawed at her insides, Jessie steeled herself for the battle ahead, praying that somehow, against all odds, she would find the strength to prevail.

Jessie's breath caught in her throat as the leader continued to circle her like a predator stalking its prey. Her heart pounded against her ribcage, each beat a desperate plea for escape. She could feel beads of sweat forming on her brow, threatening to betray her fear.

"Tell me," the leader said, his voice low and menacing, "what makes you think you can defy us?"

Jessie forced herself to meet his unnerving gaze. She swallowed hard, trying to find her voice. "I... I've faced darkness before," she stammered, attempting to mask her terror with bravado. "I won't let it consume me or those I care about."

"Ah, the power of love and friendship" – he scoffed –"such sentimental nonsense." He paused, his eyes narrowing as if he could peer into Jessie's very soul. "But that is precisely what will be your undoing."

Her fingers trembled as they curled into fists at her sides, struggling to find the courage to stand up to this enigmatic figure. In her mind's eye, she frantically searched for any possible advantage, any weakness she could exploit. But there was nothing – just an overwhelming sense of despair that threatened to suffocate her.

"Enough games," the leader announced abruptly, halting his predatory circling. "It's time for you to make a choice, Miss Jessie."

Her stomach churned as she awaited his ultimatum, knowing that either option would carry a heavy price.

"Join us" – he stared her down, a wicked smile playing on his lips –" or watch everything you love consumed by darkness. There is no middle ground."

Jessie blinked back the tears that threatened to spill over her cheeks, her heart skipping a beat as she weighed her impossible options. The air around her felt charged with anticipation, the flickering light casting eerie shadows that seemed to close in on her.

"Decide now," he ordered, his voice cold and unyielding. "Time is running out."

Jessie knew time was running out but she also knew she couldn't join forces with this abhorrent society and its leader, whoever he is. And with his chilling words ringing in her ears, Jessie feared her world would begin to crumble around her, leaving her teetering on the edge of an abyss from which there would be no return.

Deciding not to answer the leader, she turned around and walked away unharmed.

After walking several hundred yards, Jessie saw Khan. "Miss Jessie, I know you are still in shock but please let Bill and George know you are okay."

"Of course, Khan, and thank you for being there by my side."

Doubts

IN THE SAFETY OF her home, she made a telephone call to George who promised to let Bill know she was safe.

"Would you like some company?" Bill said gently.

"I am fine. I just need some rest," Jessie said.

Jessie sat alone in her study, the dim lamplight casting shadows on her pale face as she frowned at the stacks of books and papers scattered around her. Her auburn hair framed her face in loose curls, but the usually vibrant hue seemed dull and lifeless, much like her spirit at that moment.

"Am I really cut out for this?" Jessie's thoughts swirled in a tumultuous storm of doubt and uncertainty. "I've been doing this for years, but have I truly made any difference? Am I even capable of solving this case?"

Her fingers traced the spine of a thick, leather-bound book on paranormal phenomena - a topic she had become an expert in over the years. Yet, with every new piece of knowledge acquired, it felt as though there were countless more mysteries still to uncover. She sighed, her thoughts dragging her down, her slender shoulders slumping.

"Everyone thinks I'm so clever, but what do I really know about the paranormal world? It's not like I can just waltz into the spirit realm and demand answers. I'm no medium," she whispered to herself, her voice tinged with frustration.

Jessie's gaze drifted towards the window, where the moon cast a silver glow upon the city streets below. The cobblestones glistened with fresh rain, a reflection of her own turmoil mirrored in their slick surface. She thought of all those who depended on her expertise, her unique ability to communicate with and understand the spirits that haunted their lives.

"Maybe I'm not as gifted as everyone seems to think. Maybe I'm nothing more than a fraud," she mused, her heart heavy with her perceived inadequacy. "But is it enough to simply give up and walk away? What will happen to the memory of Elsie and the others if I don't find a way to help them?"

As Jessie's thoughts continued to spiral, she couldn't help but feel a growing sense of despair. She was at a crossroads, unsure of her own abilities and uncertain which path would lead her towards the truth she sought. All she knew was that she couldn't bear to let down those who counted on her most - the lost souls she had sworn to protect and guide.

"Alright, Jessie," she murmured, steeling herself for the tests ahead. "You've faced difficult times before, and you've always found a way through. This time will be no different. You have the strength and determination to see this through, no matter how impossible it may seem."

Jessie straightened her posture, her expression now etched with a readiness to do battle. She might not have all the answers just yet, but she would do everything in her power to find the truth and bring justice to those who had been wronged.

If there was one thing she knew for certain, it was that she could never truly abandon her calling as a librarian specialising in the paranormal. The spirits needed her, and she would not let them down.

Jessie's troubled eyes scanned the pages of an old tome without truly absorbing its contents. Her thoughts were elsewhere, tangled in a web of doubt and uncertainty. It was then that Khan, her faithful feline companion, entered the room.

Khan's keen senses had picked up on Jessie's distress even before he laid eyes on her. His eyes narrowed with concern as he studied his human friend, silently assessing her emotional state. The sleek black cat moved gracefully towards Jessie, his tail flicking from side to side.

"Hello, Khan," Jessie murmured, managing a weak smile as she noticed the cat approaching. "I didn't know you were around."

Khan responded with a soft meow, fixing his gaze on Jessie as if to say, 'I'm always here for you.' He made his way to her chair, leaping onto her lap in one fluid motion. Jessie could feel the warmth of Khan's body seeping through her clothes, and it brought her some small comfort.

Khan nuzzled against Jessie, purring softly as if to reassure her that everything would be alright. His comforting presence seemed to have a calming effect on her, and she felt a wave of gratitude wash over her. She closed her eyes for a moment, allowing herself to soak in that support, her hand instinctively reaching out to stroke Khan's silky fur.

"Thank you, Khan," Jessie whispered, "I don't know what I'd do without you."

Khan let out a contented purr in response, rubbing his head against Jessie's hand and meeting her eyes with an intensity that seemed to say, 'You're never alone.'

With Khan's presence, Jessie felt a calmness start to take root within her. Though her doubts still lingered, she knew that she couldn't let them hold her back any longer.

She had a duty to fulfil, not just for herself, but for the spirits that relied on her unique gifts.

"Alright then, Khan," Jessie said, taking a sharp intake of breath and meeting her feline friend's unwavering stare. "We've got work to do."

Jessie turned her attention back to the research materials spread out before her, no longer feeling quite so lost in the face of the seemingly insurmountable task that lay ahead. Together with Khan, she would face whatever challenges came their way, driven by the fierce resolve to help those who could no longer help themselves.

Jessie stroked Khan's fur, feeling the reassuring warmth of his body against her own. She looked into his eyes, searching for answers in their depths.

"Khan, do you really think I can do this?" Jessie asked hesitantly, her voice wavering as she questioned herself. "I mean, I've dealt with spirits before, but this case... it feels different. Bigger, somehow."

Khan tilted his head, considering her words carefully. He let out a gentle meow as if to say, 'Of course you can.' His unwavering belief was evident in his eyes, and his soft purr hummed like a soothing lullaby.

"Jessie," Khan seemed to communicate through his gaze alone, "you possess a rare and powerful gift. Your connection to the spirit world is unlike anything I've ever seen.

You have the strength to overcome any obstacle, no matter how daunting it may seem."

Jessie's heart swelled at Khan's reassurances, feeling as though his confidence in her abilities was seeping into her very soul, filling her with newfound confidence. She inhaled deeply allowing his words to truly sink in.

"Maybe you're right," Jessie admitted, her voice growing stronger by the moment. "I've come this far, haven't I? I can't give up now, not when so many are counting on me."

Khan nuzzled her hand and said, 'That's the spirit,' his warm breath tickled her skin. He blinked his bright green eyes slowly, a feline sign of trust and affection that only served to strengthen Jessie's resolve.

"Thank you, Khan," she whispered softly, gratitude shining in her eyes. "Your faith in me means more than you'll ever know."

With Khan's reassurance, Jessie felt ready to face whatever lay ahead. The path may be steep and full of danger, but she knew that her unique gift, coupled with the steadfast support of her feline friend and his supernatural abilities would guide her through even the darkest of nights.

"Come on, Khan," Jessie said resolutely, her voice steady and sure. "Let's get back to work."

Together, they turned their attention to the case at hand, ready to face whatever twists and turns awaited them on their journey to uncover the truth.

A warmth spread through Jessie, as if Khan's belief in her was igniting a fire within. Her fingers tapped the pages of her research, no longer trembling with doubt but steady and purposeful. She found herself sitting up straighter in her chair, her shoulders squared and her chin lifted ever so slightly.

"Khan," she said to the wise feline at her side, "let's go over all the facts we have so far." Khan tilted his head, a sign of attentiveness that Jessie found endearing.

As they delved back into their investigation, Jessie felt her thoughts becoming more focused and clearer. Each piece of evidence, each connection she made, seemed to solidify her growing confidence. The muscles in her brow relaxed, and she allowed herself to fully immerse in the process.

"Every person affected by this case deserves answers, Khan," Jessie mused aloud, her voice carrying an undertone of resolute conviction. "We're doing this for Elsie and Margaret and the other victims, and for the families who've been torn apart."

The reflection in the polished surface of her antique mahogany desk showed a woman transformed. She knew in her heart that she had a responsibility to use her gift for the greater good, to bring peace to those who'd suffered unimaginable loss.

"Remember, Khan," she whispered, her words tinged with conviction, "we're not just chasing shadows. We're shining a light on the truth, no matter how dark that truth may be."

Khan let out a soft, rumbling purr, his green eyes locked on Jessie's, conveying his unwavering support. It was as if he could sense the shift in her demeanour and was proud to witness her renewed commitment to their mission.

"Let's do this together," Jessie declared, her voice resolute. "We'll bring justice to those who've been wronged, and we'll do it with you by my side."

Jessie inhaled the scent of old leather and musty pages that filled her study. She glanced around at the stacks of books and articles on paranormal phenomena that surrounded her, evidence of her years of dedication to this field. Determination welled up within her as she realised that all the knowledge she'd accumulated had led her to this moment, to this case.

"Khan," she said, her voice strong, "we've come too far to let our doubts hold us back now."

Khan tilted his head and gave an approving chirp.

"Right, then," she continued, "Let's go over everything we know so far and piece together the puzzle. I'm certain that we have all the clues we need to solve this mystery."

With that decision firmly made, Jessie pushed herself up from her chair. Her spine straightened, and her shoulders squared, transforming her posture into one of unyielding ferocity. The previous cloud of doubt that had shrouded her face was replaced by a resolute expression, her eyes alight with a fiery conviction.

With each vibration of Khan's purr, Jessie felt her resolve grow stronger. She knew that they were more than just amateur sleuths and sidekicks; they were a united force capable of achieving the impossible. Together, they would conquer any obstacle that arose in their path and unearth the truth hidden beneath the shadows.

"Ready for the next step, partner?" Jessie asked, her eyes shining with anticipation.

Khan blinked slowly, his purr never wavering, as if to say he was ready for whatever lay ahead.

Jessie took a deep breath, feeling as if a weight had been lifted off her shoulders. The air in the study seemed to hum with possibility and newfound purpose. As she looked around the room, the once daunting books and research materials now appeared as allies in her quest for justice.

"Khan, I think it's time we paid a visit to Elsie's house," Jessie said, her voice resolute. "There must be something we've missed, some clue that will lead us to the perpetrator."

Khan responded with an affirmative flick of his tail, his eyes locked on Jessie's face and said, 'I'm with you every step of the way.'

"Good. We'll go there first thing tomorrow morning," Jessie decided, mentally preparing herself for what lay ahead. She knew that taking a look at her friend's home might bring up painful memories for those who loved Elsie, but she also understood that it was crucial to their investigation. They owed it to Elsie and the other victims to leave no stone unturned.

"Come on, Khan. Let's get some rest. Tomorrow is going to be a long day," Jessie said, the corners of her mouth lifting into a confident smile.

With one last reassuring glance at the books and papers scattered across her desk, Jessie left the study, her steps light and purposeful. She could sense that they were on the brink of a breakthrough, inching ever closer to unravelling the tangled web of this paranormal mystery.

"Tomorrow's another day, Khan," Jessie murmured, a glint in her eyes. "We'll dive deeper into this mystery and face whatever obstacles come our way."

Khan looked up at her and let out a soft meow, his emerald gaze reflecting a fierce loyalty that only deepened Jessie's resolve.

Revealed

Jessie stood at the centre of the *ad hoc* investigation team of George, her and Detective Sergeant Bill Roberts. They were in the brightly lit room at Hatton Garden police station as they pored over the cryptic evidence before them. The faint smell of mothballs clung to the air, a reminder of the musty cupboard in Elsie's home in which they had discovered the latest clue related to the cult and the connected murders.

"Look at this," said George, holding up a yellowed journal with frayed edges. "These entries go back decades, and there are mentions of rituals, sacrifices, and strange symbols."

"Could be our key to unravelling this whole sordid mess," Jessie mused, her fingers tracing the outline of a particularly ominous-looking sigil on one of the pages. Her mind raced as she tried to piece together the fragments of information they had uncovered so far.

"Jessie, I think I found something," Bill announced from across the room. His voice trembled slightly, betraying his nerves. Jessie hurried over, her heart pounding in anticipation.

"Show me," she demanded, her eyes scanning the document he held out to her. It was an old photograph of several hooded figures, their faces obscured by shadow. In the background, a familiar landmark loomed ominously.

"Isn't that...?" Jessie trailed off, unable to bring herself to say it aloud.

"It does look like it," Bill said, his tone grave. "That means we're getting closer."

Jessie looked around at the team, sensing the tension and urgency in the air. They all felt it – the unspoken understanding that they were on the precipice of uncovering something monumental. A major revelation lurked just beyond their grasp, and each new piece of evidence brought them one step closer to grasping it.

"Alright, everyone," Jessie declared, trying to quell the anxious energy coursing through her. "We need to dig deeper. Follow every lead, no matter how insignificant it may seem. Time is of the essence, and I have a feeling that we're running out of it."

Her team nodded in agreement, filled with a common shared will power as they returned to their respective tasks.

As Jessie bent back over the journal, her mind racing with possibilities, she couldn't shake the gnawing feeling that they were on the verge of something much bigger than any of them could have anticipated.

"Jessie," George said quietly, drawing her attention to another document he'd found. "Look at this list of names. Some of them are victims; others are people who came to our notice at the council."

"Are you suggesting they might all be connected?" Jessie asked, her voice barely above a whisper as the implications of his discovery set in.

"It's possible," he replied, his brow furrowed in concentration. "We need to follow up on this and see where it leads us."

"Agreed," Jessie said firmly, her resolve hardening. She knew they were close to uncovering the truth, but she also knew it would come at a cost. As she looked around at the team, each one diligently working to unravel the mystery before them, she steeled herself for whatever lay ahead. The stakes had never been higher, and they couldn't afford to make any mistakes – not with lives hanging in the balance.

Jessie's fingers trembled as she leafed through the pile of documents, her eyes scanning the pages with a rising sense of horror. The evidence was undeniable now, laid out in cold ink before her: Elsie, her dear departed friend; her husband, Richard, was the secret society's leader. He was the Hawk.

"Look at this," she said, her voice hoarse as she held up a letter bearing Richard's signature. "He's giving orders to the other members."

"Bloody hell... excuse my French," George muttered under his breath, staring at the paper in disbelief. Jessie and Bill exchanged grim looks, their faces pale.

"Jessie, are you alright?" George asked, concern etching his features.

"Fine," Jessie gritted out, though her stomach churned violently, and her heart thudded painfully. "I'm fine."

But she wasn't. She couldn't be. How could she think of Elsie the same way again, knowing that her husband was responsible for so much pain and suffering? And how could she reconcile the man she'd laughed with at dinner parties, who had seemed so kind and charming, with the monster he truly was?

Jessie was desperate for fresh air. She headed for the door and paced outside the police station with her mind in turmoil. Finding a secluded spot, she heard a familiar voice, "Miss Jessie, I'm here if you need to talk," Khan said.

"Oh! Khan, I feel such a fool. Why didn't I recognise Richard as the leader from the earlier encounters?"

"He used spells. Don't you recall the time you thought you had killed him, he crumbled to dust. Richard must have changed his appearance and his voice the second time. I must concede he seems to be a powerful wizard," Khan said.

"Poor Elsie," Jessie said.

"Indeed, you didn't know him because of his evil wizardry but Elsie didn't truly know the man she married," Khan said.

"Khan, you are so wise. That's exactly why she hid that journal in the cupboard at her home in case something terrible happened to her and it did, of course."

"Jessie," Khan said gently, placing a paw on her shoulder. "We're going to get through this. We'll bring him to justice, and we'll put an end to this madness."

"Yes, we are. Let's get back inside. We have much to do," Jessie said.

BACK INSIDE THE POLICE station Khan became invisible once more whilst Bill and George fussed over Jessie. Bill was the first to speak.

"Jessie," Bill chimed in, his gravelly voice unwavering. "Whatever you're feeling, it's normal. But remember, we stand united."

She nodded, drawing in a shaky breath. The room seemed to close in around her, the scent of old paper and musty files pervading her nostrils. Her thoughts raced and images of Richard's smiling face haunted her mind as she tried to reconcile his dual nature.

"Let's keep digging," Jessie said, her voice fierce as she sought to regain control of her emotions. "We need to find out everything we can about this society and how they've been operating."

Jessie vowed that Richard would pay for his crimes. And if that meant tearing down everything she thought she knew about him, then so be it.

The air in the CID office seemed to hum with tension as Detective Sergeant Bill Roberts and the team absorbed the revelation of Elsie's husband being the leader of the secret society. George, who had always been a man of few words, stared blankly at the scattered documents on the table, his fingers drumming nervously on the edge. Bill rubbed at his temples, an unspoken weariness etched in the lines of his face. Even the invisible Khan, the stoic protector of the group, looked as if he'd been blindsided by a fierce gust of wind.

"Can't believe it." George shook his head, finally breaking the silence. "Richard? Bloody hell, this changes everything."

"Indeed," Bill said, his voice heavy. "It's one thing to be investigating a secret society, but it's another to find out that one of us is personally connected to their leader."

Jessie clenched her fists, nails digging into her palm. She couldn't allow herself to wallow in shock and disbelief any longer. There was too much at stake here – the lives that had already been lost and the potential for more victims if they didn't act quickly.

"Listen," Jessie said, her voice steady and strong despite the storm brewing inside her. "We need to focus on the task at hand. Richard may have fooled us all, but we can't let that distract us from bringing him and his followers to justice."

"Right," George agreed, giving Jessie a supportive nod. "We can't afford to lose sight of our goal, no matter how personal it's become."

"Exactly," she continued, addressing her team. "Our first priority is to ensure that no one else falls victim to this cult. If that means confronting someone I once considered a friend, then so be it."

Her words seemed to galvanise the others, their expressions hardening with resolve. They knew what was at stake, and they were prepared to face it head-on, together.

"Jessie's right," Bill said, looking at her with a newfound respect. "We need to focus on stopping these killers and preventing any more harm from coming to innocent people."

"Agreed," George chimed in, his expression grim but steadfast. "I don't know how Richard could do this, but we owe it to Elsie and the others to make sure he pays for what he's done."

"Then let's get to work," Jessie declared, her gaze unwavering as she stared at each of her team members. "We'll expose this cult for what it is and put an end to its reign of terror."

The team began sifting through the evidence once more, fuelled by their collective efforts to confront the darkness lurking in their midst. Together, they would bring justice to the victims and ensure that Elsie's husband could no longer wield his sinister power over the unsuspecting residents of Liverpool.

Jessie looked around the table at the team, their faces illuminated by the soft glow of a table lamp in Bill's office. She could see the sense of purpose in their eyes, but also the fear that lingered beneath the surface.

"Alright," Jessie began, taking a deep breath as she prepared to address the team. "We need to come up with a plan to confront Richard and his followers. We can't just waltz in there unprepared."

Bill leaned forward, his brow furrowed in thought. "We'll need to gather more information about the inner workings of the society – any weaknesses or vulnerabilities we can exploit."

"Agreed," George chimed in, tapping his fingers on the table. "If we can find a way to infiltrate their inner circle, perhaps we can gather enough evidence to take them down from the inside."

"A clandestine operation?" Bill mused, stroking his chin thoughtfully. "It's risky, but it might be our best shot at getting close to Richard without raising suspicion."

Jessie nodded, considering their options. Her thoughts raced as she weighed the risks and rewards of each possible course of action. "We'll need to be careful, though," she cautioned. "I don't want anyone else getting hurt because of this. We're going to have to be smart about how we approach this."

"Jessie, you can count on us," Bill reassured her, placing a hand on her shoulder. "We're in this together, and we'll do whatever it takes to put an end to this nightmare."

"Thank you," Jessie replied, a small smile tugging at the corners of her mouth. "It means the world to me to know that I have all of you by my side." At that point, she gave Khan a sideways glimpse to ensure he knew he was included.

"Let's focus on gathering information first," George suggested, pulling out a map of the city they had been using to trace the society's movements. "If we can identify their key locations and personnel, it'll give us a better chance of getting inside without being detected."

"Good idea," Jessie agreed. "We'll need to divide and conquer – each of us can take a different area of the city to investigate."

"Jessie, I think you should focus on Richard," Bill interjected, his eyes filled with concern. "You know him best, and you're the one who discovered his involvement in all this. It's only right that you be the one to confront him."

Jessie hesitated for a moment, her heart pounding at the thought of facing Richard – the man she had once considered a friend. But she knew that Bill was right. This was her responsibility, and she would see it through to the end. Besides, she knew Khan would be there right at her side.

"Alright," she agreed, determination hardening her features. "I'll confront Richard. But we need to work together as a team to ensure our plan is airtight."

"Of course, Jessie," George assured her, his voice steady and resolute.

With the plan in place, Jessie and her team spent the next few hours preparing for the final confrontation. Each of them knew the gravity of the situation and the importance of their roles in bringing justice to the victims.

The team decided to retire to Jessie's flat to prepare for what was to come.

Jessie stood before the full-length mirror in her bedroom, studying her reflection. Her hair was pulled back into a tight bun, ensuring it wouldn't obstruct her vision during the fight. She wore all black, the fabric clinging to her lean frame – a silent, deadly shadow ready to strike. For a moment, she let her mind wander to the days when Elsie's husband, Richard, was just a friend. The betrayal stung, but she pushed the memories aside, steeling herself for what lay ahead.

"Are you ready?" Khan asked as he entered the room, his voice steady but betraying a hint of apprehension.

"I'm as ready as I'll ever be," Jessie replied, meeting his gaze in the mirror. "This ends tonight, one way or another."

Khan nodded solemnly, placing a reassuring paw on her leg. "We will succeed, Jessie – never forget that."

In the living room, George and Bill were double-checking their supplies: pocket torches, rope, and a small arsenal of makeshift weapons they hoped would give them an edge in any upcoming battle.

"Alright, everyone," Jessie called out, her voice filled with resolve. "Let's do this."

She joined them in the living room and as they shared a knowing glance, Jessie could see the unspoken promise between them – they would stand by her, come what may.

Bill drove to the hidden cult's lair. It was a tense journey, each member of the team was lost in their thoughts, mentally preparing themselves for the ordeal ahead. As they parked the car and approached the entrance to the underground hideout, the air seemed to thicken with anticipation.

"Stay sharp," Jessie warned, "We don't know what we'll find in there."

With a nod from each of them, Jessie led her team into the darkness, their torch beams cutting through the gloom as they descended into the bowels of the lair. The walls were adorned with disturbing symbols and grotesque artwork, hinting at the twisted nature of the group they sought to dismantle.

"Jessie," George whispered, his eyes wide with apprehension. "I've never seen anything like this before."

"Me neither," she admitted, her heart hammering. "But we can't let fear control us now. Those people – the victims – they're counting on us."

As they ventured deeper into the lair, the sound of chanting reached their ears, growing louder and more ominous with each step. Suddenly, they found themselves facing a large, ornate door, the sinister markings on its surface leaving no doubt that they had found the heart of the secret society.

"Ready?" Jessie asked, her knuckles white as she gripped a makeshift weapon tightly. Each member of her team nodded, their faces set with a firmness of purpose.

"Yes," Bill said quietly, his voice laced with equal parts courage and trepidation.

Together, they pushed open the door, stepping into the hidden chamber where Elsie's husband and his followers awaited them, seemingly prepared for the confrontation. The atmosphere was electric, charged with the potential for violence and the promise of justice.

"Richard," Jessie called out, her voice unwavering. "It's time to end this."

Fire and Adversity

THE ROOM ERUPTED INTO chaos as Jessie and the team clashed with the cult in a frenzy of violence. The air was thick with tension, every strike and parry fuelled by the principles of justice and vengeance. Jessie's makeshift weapon found its mark, felling one opponent after another, whilst George and Bill fought ferociously alongside her. Khan, again invisible, had taken on the strength of a tiger and destroyed all the society members who got in his way.

"Jessie, watch out!" Bill shouted as a cloaked figure lunged towards her with a dagger. She ducked under the blade and retaliated with a swift blow to their assailant's stomach. Gritting her teeth, she pushed aside the memories of betrayal that threatened to cloud her focus.

"Stay together!" George called out, using his cane as a weapon and connecting with an enemy's midsection.

Through this chaos, Jessie scanned the battlefield for Elsie's husband, Richard.

Finally spotting him, standing still amidst the bedlam, Jessie's heart clenched. But she was no longer the woman who had crumbled under the act of betrayal and who had doubted her abilities. She had grown stronger, braver – forged through fire and adversity.

"Richard!" she called out, striding towards him. His eyes met hers, cold and unyielding, but she refused to be intimidated.

"Jessie." He sneered, a twisted smile playing on his lips. "Did you really think you could stop us?"

"Watch me," she countered, her voice steady despite the turmoil within her. Her newfound confidence propelled her forward, ready to confront the man who had betrayed not only her trust but also the lives of countless innocent people.

"Your misplaced faith in humanity will be your downfall," Richard taunted, a cruel glint in his eyes as he raised his weapon. "But I suppose you've learned that the hard way, haven't you?"

"It's not misplaced," Jessie retorted, her grip tightening on her weapon. "I believe in the strength and goodness of my friends – something you'll never understand."

"Friends?" Richard scoffed, launching himself at her with a vicious swing. "They'll only ever let you down."

Jessie parried his blow effortlessly, her newfound confidence shining through in every deft movement. "That's where you're wrong, Richard. They will always be there for me, just like I will be for them."

As their weapons clashed once more, Jessie knew she was no longer the same woman who had first encountered this dark world. She had grown, evolved, and found the courage to stand up against those who sought to harm others. And with her team, she knew they would bring justice to the victims, no matter the cost.

The room shook with the force of their blows, the air thick with tension as Jessie and the team fought relentlessly against the cult members. The cold stone floor echoed with every desperate struggle, footfalls landing heavily as each combatant sought to gain the upper hand.

Unseen and unheard by all except Jessie, Khan shouted, "Take that!" as he subdued one of the assailants, his eyes never leaving the next target.

George and Bill worked in tandem, their years of friendship and soldiering allowing them to anticipate one another's movements, dismantling their opponents with swift efficiency.

Amidst the chaos, Jessie found herself locked in a fierce duel with Elsie's husband, Richard. Their weapons struck together with a resounding clang, beads of sweat gathering on Jessie's forehead as she focused all her strength into each deft parry and counterstrike. She could feel her heart pounding, but it wasn't fear that drove her now – it was determination and newfound confidence.

"Give up, Richard!" Jessie bellowed, her voice ringing clear above the din of battle. "You've lost."

Richard snarled, his face contorted with rage. But despite his fury, Jessie could see the flicker of doubt in his eyes. At that moment, she knew they had him cornered.

"Never!" he spat, lunging forward with renewed vigour. But Jessie was ready for him. With a fluid motion, she sidestepped his attack and brought her weapon down upon his, disarming him with a shattering impact.

As Richard stumbled back, gasping for breath, Jessie turned to survey the room. Her teammates stood victorious, the remaining members of the secret society either unconscious or cowering before them.

"Jessie," George panted, wiping blood from a small cut on his forehead. "We did it. We stopped them."

Jessie nodded, her chest swelling with pride. "Yes, we did."

They had done more than just foil the schemes of a twisted secret society. Together, they had solved the murders that had plagued their community and brought justice to the victims and their families. The significance of their victory settled upon Jessie like a warm embrace, filling her with a sense of purpose and accomplishment.

"Jessie," George said quietly, his gaze locked on the defeated figure of Elsie's husband. "What do we do with him?"

"Turn him over to the authorities," Jessie replied without hesitation. "No one is above the law."

As Bill handcuffed Richard, Jessie stared at the man who had once held her trust. She felt no sympathy for him, only the cold satisfaction of knowing he would pay for his crimes. It was a far cry from the naive woman she had been – the one who believed in the inherent goodness of all people, even those who wore the mask of friendship.

"Let's get out of here," Jessie said. "We've got justice to deliver."

THE BATTLE MAY HAVE been won, but the war was far from over. As Jessie and her team left the hidden lair, she knew their fight for justice had only just begun. But together, they were unstoppable. And whatever darkness awaited them, they would face it head-on, united as one.

The sun dipped low on the horizon, casting a warm glow over the city as Jessie and her team stood on the rooftop of a nearby building, surveying the aftermath of their victory. The breeze carried with it the scent of justice, and for the first time in ages, Jessie felt a sense of peace settle within her.

"Hard to believe it's all over," George remarked, his voice tinged with both relief and apprehension. He looked out at the cityscape, the setting sun casting elongated shadows on the buildings below.

"Indeed," Jessie agreed, her gaze flicking towards Elsie's husband, who was now in police custody. "But we've done what needed to be done."

"Jessie," Bill chimed in, his eyes filled with understanding as he placed a supportive hand on her shoulder. "You showed incredible strength today. We're proud of you."

Jessie allowed herself a small smile, her heart swelling with gratitude for her loyal friends. "Thank you, but I couldn't have done it without all of you."

"Here's to teamwork," George said, raising an imaginary toast in the air. They shared a moment of camaraderie, the bond between them stronger than ever.

As the sun disappeared beneath the horizon, Jessie's thoughts drifted to the future. The world was still riddled with darkness, but they had proven that light could prevail. It wouldn't be easy, but she knew they were up for the challenge.

"Any idea what comes next?" George asked, breaking the silence that had settled around them.

"More mysteries to solve, more secrets to uncover," Jessie replied, her eyes sparkling with determination. "We'll keep fighting for justice, for the innocent and for those who can't defend themselves."

"Sounds like a good idea to me," Bill grinned, clapping Jessie on the back. "Let's get some rest and then start fresh tomorrow."

"Agreed," Jessie nodded, her thoughts already swirling with the possibilities of what lay ahead. She knew there would be more battles to fight, and more hidden evils to confront, but she also knew that together, they could overcome anything.

Khan, ever discreet, stayed invisible apart from a split second when he winked at Jessie. With one last look at the fading light of day, Jessie turned and followed the team back down from the rooftop, ready to embrace a new day. United in their shared purpose, they stepped into the twilight, the promise of a brighter tomorrow guiding their way.

A Dream

In police custody, some of Richard's followers explained how he had put them under a spell to carry out his commands including the murders of Elsie, his wife, and the three other victims. All the victims had threatened to expose the secret society and the corruption within the council. The corruption involved illegal payments to obtain construction permits and involved Richard and Councillor Thompson. Thompson was also a secret society member.

Jessie didn't believe these claims but was resigned to the fact they would almost certainly convict Richard of these heinous crimes. In the safety of her own home, her thoughts once more turned to Margaret who unbeknown to Jessie had disappeared before the confrontation with the society and the arrests.

Jessie's heart felt like a ship lost at sea, tossed about by waves of betrayal and disappointment. Margaret's unfathomable actions had left her reeling, and she felt as if the ground beneath her had shifted, leaving her unsteady and unsure of whom to trust.

"Is everything alright, Jessie?" Khan asked with concern, noticing the distress in his friend's eyes.

Jessie shook her head slowly, her auburn curls catching the light as they danced around her shoulders. "No," she admitted, hesitating before confiding in him. "I just can't understand why Margaret had been involved with the society we've been investigating. I feel so... hurt."

Khan's dark eyes softened with empathy. "It is never easy to learn that someone close to you has betrayed your trust. But remember, Jessie, forgiveness is a powerful tool."

"Forgiveness?" Jessie raised an eyebrow, the word feeling foreign on her lips. "How can I forgive someone who willingly hurt me?"

"Because humans are imperfect creatures," Khan replied gently. "We all make mistakes, and sometimes those mistakes cause pain to others." He paused for a moment, allowing Jessie to absorb his words. "But it is how we grow from those mistakes, and how we support each other through them, that truly defines our character."

Jessie looked into Khan's eyes, feeling the importance of his wisdom. She knew he was right, but part of her still rebelled against the idea of forgiving Margaret so easily despite what she had told her in the meeting at the secret garden. Yet, she also knew that she couldn't let this fester within her; it would only bring more pain and darkness.

"Alright," she said finally, her voice trembling slightly with emotion. "I'll try to forgive her. But how do I even begin?"

"By opening your heart to understanding," Khan advised. "Identify with Margaret's side of the story and try to see things from her perspective. You may find that there's more to her actions than you initially realised."

Jessie nodded, feeling a small spark of hope amidst the stormy seas of her emotions. She knew it wouldn't be easy, but with Khan's guidance and support, she felt ready to face Margaret again and attempt the difficult task of forgiveness.

"Thank you, Khan," Jessie murmured, gratitude warming her heart. "I don't know what I'd do without your wisdom and friendship."

Khan smiled warmly, his eyes twinkling like stars in the night sky. "And I am grateful for your courage and steadfastness, Jessie. Together, we can navigate any challenge that comes our way."

Jessie steeled herself for the upcoming confrontation, bolstered by the strength of her friendship with Khan. It was time to face the unknown, and hopefully, find a path toward healing and understanding.

As Jessie left Khan's comforting presence, she found herself wandering the familiar cobblestone streets of Liverpool, deep in thought. The sun was setting, casting a soft glow on the buildings that lined the path. She paused for a moment, taking in the surroundings and allowing it to soothe her troubled heart.

"Jessie!" a voice called out, jolting her from her reverie. Turning, she saw George and Bill approaching her – two friends who had been with her since the beginning of this paranormal investigation. George, a tall man with a trim moustache and twinkling eyes, always seemed ready to crack a joke or offer a supportive hug. Bill, on the other hand, was shorter and had the beginnings of a beer belly, his sharp intellect evident in the intensity of his gaze.

"Hey, you two," Jessie greeted them, attempting a smile despite the turmoil within her. "What brings you here?"

"We thought you might need some company," George replied gently, his eyes expressing concern. "We just wanted to make sure you're alright."

"Is there anything we can do to help?" Bill chimed in, his voice was soft and earnest.

Jessie hesitated, touched by their loyalty and friendship. "I'm... struggling," she admitted in a whisper. "Margaret's betrayal has left me feeling so lost and hurt, and I don't know if I'll ever be able to forgive her."

"Jessie," Bill said gently, placing a hand on her shoulder, "it's natural to feel hurt in these situations. But remember, forgiveness is a process — it takes time and effort."

"And we're here for you every step of the way," George added, his eyes full of warmth and sincerity. "You don't have to go through this alone."

"Thank you," Jessie murmured, fighting back tears at their unwavering support. "I don't know what I'd do without you two."

"Lean on us, Jessie," Bill encouraged, giving her shoulder a reassuring squeeze. "We'll navigate this storm together."

"Besides," George said with a grin, attempting to lighten the mood, "what's an investigation without a few bumps along the way, eh?"

Jessie chuckled at his attempt at humour. Yes, she thought, these two have always been there for me, even in the darkest of times.

"Alright," Jessie said, feeling the warmth of her friends' presence. "Let's try and find Margaret and try to put things right once and for all."

"Lead the way, Jessie," George agreed, his smile warm and encouraging.

As they walked side by side, Jessie felt her despair slowly lifting, replaced by a sense of hope and real purpose. With George and Bill, and not forgetting Khan, she knew that no challenge was insurmountable – not even the daunting task of forgiving a betrayal. As they approached a small park, Jessie paused to take in the sight before her. Children played on the swings, their laughter resonating like a joyful melody. Couples strolled hand in hand, while a group of elderly men played a friendly game of chess beneath an ancient oak tree. It was a scene of love, life, and friendship. A testament to the resilience of the human spirit.

"I'm so grateful for everything we've experienced together," Jessie mused, her gaze lingering on the park's vibrant colours. "All the mysteries we've solved, the secrets we've uncovered... I wouldn't trade those memories for anything."

"Nor would we," George agreed, his eyes twinkling with sincerity.

"Besides," Bill added, a mischievous twinkle in his eye, "we're just getting started, right?"

"Right," Jessie echoed, her smile growing. She felt a surge of gratitude for the friends she had gained through this testing experience, and as they continued their walk, arm in arm, she knew that together, they could conquer anything life threw their way.

THE FOLLOWING MORNING, THE sun painted the sky in hues of pink and orange, casting a soft glow on the cobblestone streets of Liverpool. The city was stirring to life, with shopkeepers opening their doors and the distant sound of the docks' hustle and bustle. Jessie, George, and Bill had agreed to meet at a quaint café just around the corner from Jessie's flat—a place they'd come to consider their unofficial headquarters during their investigations.

As Jessie approached the café, she caught sight of her colleagues already seated at their favourite table by the window. Her heart swelled with warmth as she observed their animated conversation, their laughter echoing through the crisp morning air. She pushed open the door, the bell overhead announcing her arrival, and the familiar scent of freshly brewed coffee and warm pastries enveloped her senses.

"Ah, there she is! Our fearless leader!" Bill called out, raising his cup in salute. George chuckled, nodding in agreement.

"Good morning, you two," Jessie greeted them, taking her seat across from her trusted friends. "What were you discussing so animatedly?"

"Nothing much," George replied, stroking his moustache thoughtfully. "We were just chatting about what our next move should be, considering everything that transpired."

Jessie mulled over their words. She knew that moving forward meant leaving behind the pain Margaret had caused her. It also meant learning to trust again, not only in her friends but in herself.

"Whatever it is, we'll figure it out together," Jessie said resolutely, meeting their gazes with determination. "We've overcome challenges before, and we'll do it again."

"Agreed," George said, reaching over to clasp her hand reassuringly. "We're here for you, Jessie, every step of the way."

"Thanks, chaps," Jessie murmured, touched by their unwavering support. As she sipped her coffee, the comforting warmth spread through her body, mirroring the feeling of camaraderie that surrounded her.

"Speaking of next moves," Bill interjected, pulling out a crumpled newspaper from his coat pocket. "I came across this article about some strange happenings in the city—a possible lead for us to follow."

"Really?" Jessie asked, curiosity piqued. She leaned forward to examine the paper, her mind already racing with possibilities.

"Let's delve into it, shall we?" George suggested, excitement lighting up his eyes. George and Bill huddled around the table, their heads bowed together as they began discussing their potential new case.

"Slow down, chaps," Jessie said, "I don't know about you but I need some breathing space before I even think about the future or if I can cope with more cases."

Despite Jessie urging caution, their spirited conversation carried on, punctuated by laughter and thoughtful silences, while the café bustled around them. As they delved into the newspaper mystery, Jessie felt grateful for the steadfast friendships she had formed. With George and Bill, she knew they could navigate any challenges that lay ahead, anchored by their shared expertise and unwavering mutual trust.

The sun continued to rise, painting the sky in brilliant shades of gold and blue. A new day was dawning, filled with promise and possibility, and together, they were ready to embrace it.

Leaving the café and strolling in the nearby Sefton Park, Jessie felt the warmth of the sun on her face as she sat in the quaint park, a slight breeze rustling the leaves overhead. The sound of birdsong filled the air, creating a soothing atmosphere that seemed to reflect the inner peace she had been seeking. She closed her eyes and inhaled the fragrant scent of the nearby rose garden.

"Jessie, are you alright?" George asked gently, his concern evident in his voice.

"Thank you, George," she replied, opening her eyes to meet his gaze. "I'm just... taking it all in."

"Life certainly has a way of throwing us the unexpected," Bill chimed in with a sympathetic smile, patting Jessie's hand reassuringly.

"Indeed, it does," Jessie agreed, her thoughts drifting back to Margaret and the rollercoaster of emotions their recent confrontation had stirred up. A mix of hurt, disappointment, and forgiveness swirled within her, making her feel both vulnerable and strangely empowered.

"Forgiveness is never easy," Khan had told her just hours before. "But it's necessary for healing, for growth."

"Well, I'll be blowed, here comes Margaret," George announced, nodding towards the approaching figure. Jessie's heart skipped a beat, but she drew strength from the presence of her trusted friends by her side.

As the woman drew closer, Jessie saw she wasn't Margaret but did closely resemble her. The desire to forgive Margaret was overwhelming and Jessie saw and heard this conversation play out in her mind's eye.

"Margaret, I forgive you," Jessie declared, surprising even herself with the sincerity in her voice. "But our friendship needs to be built on trust and honesty moving forward."

"Thank you, Jessie," Margaret whispered, relief washing over her features. "I promise, from now on, I'll be completely transparent with you."

"Friends?" Jessie held out her hand. Margaret took it without hesitation, their fingers intertwining in a symbol of renewed trust.

"Friends," Margaret confirmed, smiling through her tears.

Jessie snapped out of her trance on hearing George say, "Alright, then. Let's put this behind us and move forward as a team."

"Agreed," Bill added, raising an imaginary cup in a toast. "To friendship and new beginnings!"

Jessie, George and Bill clinked their imaginary cups together, laughter bubbling up amidst the sound of nature's symphony around them. As Jessie allowed herself to bask in the joy of the moment, she knew that they were stronger together, ready to face whatever mysteries lay ahead.

Khan noted Jessie's dream and relayed it to the spirit world for Margaret's benefit.

Epilogue

THE KARDOMAH CAFÉ WAS filled with the hum of contented chatter and clinking porcelain as Jessie and George settled into a cosy corner, their backs pressed against the worn velvet cushions. Light from the late afternoon sun streamed through the window, casting a soft glow on their faces. They sipped at their cups of steaming tea, the fragrant scent of Earl Grey mingling with the aroma of brewed coffee, toasted crumpets and butter that wafted in from the kitchen.

"Ah, this is just what I needed," Jessie sighed, her auburn hair shimmering in the sunlight as she leaned back in her seat. "I can't believe it's all over, George."

"Me neither," he replied, his eyes crinkling with a smile. "But we did it, Jessie. We brought those rogues to justice."

She took a moment to reflect on their recent success. It felt like a lifetime ago that they'd stumbled upon the cult, a dangerous web of lies and deceit that had threatened to engulf them both. But together, they had navigated its treacherous depths and emerged victorious.

"Remember how it all started?" Jessie mused, taking a delicate sip of her tea. "We were just kids who knew each other then got thrown together by chance and look at us now. We've become quite the team, haven't we?"

George chuckled. "That we have. And we couldn't have done it without each other. You know, I never thought I was capable of something like this. But you... you have a real knack for it, Jessie. Your instincts are spot-on."

Jessie felt a flush creeping up her neck, but she knew he was right. She may not have been posh, but she was sharp as a tack. Her life in Liverpool had given her an edge, a resourcefulness that had served them well during their investigation. And George, with his calm demeanour and quick wit, had provided the perfect counterbalance to her fiery determination.

"Thank you, George," she replied softly, feeling a swell of pride at his praise. "And I couldn't have done it without you."

As they sat there, basking in the glow of their accomplishment, Jessie realised that this was more than just a moment of triumph. It was the beginning of a new chapter in her life – one where she could embrace her unique talents and make a real difference in the world. And with George, she knew that anything was possible.

The clink of porcelain cups and saucers filled the air as Jessie took a sip of her tea. She noticed the steam rising from George's cup, swirling in the warm atmosphere of the Kardomah café. She couldn't help but feel a sense of contentment wash over her as they sat there, relishing the success of their latest achievement.

"Jessie! George!" A familiar Welsh accent boomed through the chatter of the café patrons. Detective Sergeant Bill Roberts strode toward them, his burly frame and broad shoulders commanding attention. He approached their table with a grin that stretched from ear to ear, his eyes sparkling with admiration. "Everyone has heard about your success in bringing down that secret society. Congratulations are certainly in order."

"Thank you, Bill, and don't be modest. You played a huge part too," Jessie replied, returning his smile. Her heart swelled with pride at the recognition from someone she considered not only a mentor but also a friend.

"Please, have a seat," George offered, gesturing to an empty chair. Bill obliged and joined them at the table, his excitement palpable.

"Really, you two have done an incredible job," Bill said earnestly, leaning forward in his chair. "You've both shown exceptional skill and dedication throughout this entire investigation. It's truly impressive."

A blush crept up Jessie's cheeks as she demurely lowered her gaze to her teacup. She felt the warmth of George's hand on hers and gave it a reassuring squeeze. They had indeed accomplished something extraordinary and hearing it from Bill only solidified the truth of it.

"Actually," Bill continued, his tone growing more serious, "I've been thinking... With talents like yours, you two should consider opening your own private investigation agency. You make a formidable team, and I believe there's a real demand for people with your skills."

George's eyebrows raised in surprise, but he didn't dismiss the idea outright. Instead, he exchanged a glance with Jessie, as if gauging her reaction. Her heart raced at the prospect – could they really make a go of it, continuing to solve mysteries like the one they'd just conquered?

"Bill," Jessie said slowly, weighing her words, "that's an interesting idea. We've certainly proven that we can work well together." She looked over at George, seeking his input.

"Indeed," George agreed, a thoughtful expression on his face. "It's not something I had considered before, but perhaps it's worth exploring."

As Jessie mulled over Bill's suggestion, she felt a surge of excitement course through her. This could be the opportunity she'd been waiting for – a chance to truly embrace her unique talents and make a difference in the world. And with George by her side, she knew they could succeed.

Jessie hesitated, her fingers drumming on the table as she contemplated Bill's words. A wave of doubt washed over her, and she couldn't help but question if she was truly capable of running an agency and taking on more cases. The idea was thrilling, but it also seemed so daunting.

"Bill, I appreciate your confidence in us," Jessie admitted, her voice wavering slightly. "But do you really think we can handle something like that? Running our own agency?" Her gaze flickered between George and Bill, seeking reassurance.

As if sensing her uncertainty, Khan, her ever-present feline companion, made his presence known. He nudged her hand gently with his paw, purring softly as he gazed up at her with his wise green eyes. The familiar warmth of his fur against her skin brought a small smile to her face; throughout their adventures, Khan had been an unwavering source of emotional support for Jessie. His presence reminded her of her unique gift and the strength she had shown time and time again.

"Jessie," George said, his voice steady and reassuring, "we've faced incredible difficulties together, and we've come out on top every time. You have a talent for this, and I believe in you."

She looked down at Khan, who continued to purr contentedly, his eyes never leaving hers. It was as if he was trying to tell her that everything would be alright, that they could face whatever came their way.

"Thank you, George," Jessie whispered, feeling some of her self-doubt ebbing away. She took a deep breath, her resolve growing stronger by the second. "Alright, let's talk about what we'd need to make this happen."

As they delved into the logistics of opening a private investigation agency, Jessie felt her confidence building. With the support of her friends – both human and feline – she knew they could achieve anything they set their minds to. For the first time in a long while, Jessie allowed herself to dream of a future where her unique abilities would be put to good use, solving mysteries and helping others, one case at a time.

The steam from their cups of tea curled up into the air like tendrils, wrapping around Jessie and George as they sat in the cosy corner of the Kardomah Café. George's voice was a soothing balm to Jessie's nerves as he spoke with conviction.

"Jessie, I have no doubt that we make a fantastic team," he said, his eyes gleaming with unwavering belief in her abilities. "You're a natural-born leader, and I have complete faith in you."

Jessie felt a flutter of warmth in her chest, but she hesitated, absentmindedly stirring her tea. Khan, sensing her turmoil, stretched out on her lap, his purr a reassuring vibration against her legs. The café's chatter seemed to fade into a distant murmur as she focused on George's words and the comforting presence of her feline companion.

"Really, George?" She asked, searching for any hint of uncertainty in his expression. But all she saw was resolute confidence.

Her eyes flicked to Khan, who gazed back at her with steadfast loyalty. With every memory George recounted, Jessie could sense her previous feelings of self-doubt beginning to lift. It was true; they had faced seemingly insurmountable problems together and always came out victorious. Perhaps it was time to embrace this new chapter and finally put her unique gifts to good use.

"Alright," Jessie said, "Perhaps we can do this."

George's smile lit up his face, and even Khan seemed to purr louder as if he approved of her newfound resolve. At that moment, Jessie knew that with the help of her friends, everything was possible. Together, they would forge a new path and continue their thrilling adventures, one mystery at a time.

Jessie's fingers traced the rim of her teacup, lost in thought as she considered the practicalities of opening a detective agency. The steam from the tea had left a faint mist on the café window, blurring the bustling street outside. She glanced at George, who was eagerly sketching potential office layouts on a napkin.

"First things first," George said, eyes alight with excitement. "We'll need a suitable office space, somewhere central and easily accessible. I've seen a few promising places near here in Dale Street."

Jessie nodded, tapping her chin thoughtfully. "And we'll need to apply for the necessary licences, won't we? I'm sure there must be some kind of private investigator's permit or something."

"Absolutely," George replied, his pen never ceasing its frantic dance across the paper. "I can research the requirements and handle all the paperwork. You should focus on honing your skills and building our reputation in the community."

Jessie smiled gratefully, feeling the warm camaraderie between them. She knew she could rely on George to handle the logistical side of things, while she continued to strengthen their connections and solve even more mysteries. It was a perfect partnership.

"Thank you, George," Jessie said, her voice thick with emotion. "I don't know what I would do without you."

"Same here, Jessie," he replied, looking up from his drawings with a sincere smile. "We make quite the team, don't we?"

They shared a quiet chuckle, their laughter mingling with the murmurs of other patrons and the clinking of silverware. Jessie felt a profound sense of gratitude for the friends who believed in her, even when she doubted herself.

"Speaking of teamwork," Jessie began, turning her attention to Bill, who had been listening intently to their plans. "We couldn't have accomplished any of this without your support and guidance, Bill. If you're ever looking for a change of pace from the police force, we'd be honoured to have you as a consultant at our agency."

Bill's eyes widened in surprise, but a broad grin soon spread across his face. "You never know, Jessie, but I do have my pension to think of," he said. "Don't you fret though, I'll keep an eye on the new agency."

"With or without you, Bill!" George exclaimed, raising his teacup in a toast. "To new beginnings and continued success!"

The trio clinked their cups together, their faces alight with enthusiasm and anticipation. And as Jessie sipped her tea, she felt a gentle nudge from Khan, who had settled on her lap, purring his approval.

Jessie smiled, touched by Bill's sincerity and dedication. She glanced at George, whose eyes sparkled with anticipation, and then down at Khan, who continued to purr softly on her lap.

"Then it's settled," Jessie announced, her voice filled with determination. "We'll join forces and bring justice to those who need it most."

As they raised their teacups once more, Jessie envisioned the adventures that lay ahead. The challenges they would face, the secrets they would uncover, and the unbreakable bond they would forge as a team. Her heart swelled with pride, knowing that she had found her true calling alongside her closest friends.

"Here's to uncovering the truth, no matter where it leads us," George added, his voice filled with equal parts excitement and resolve.

Their cups clinked together, sealing their toast and their commitment to one another. As they sipped their tea, Jessie felt an unfamiliar sense of peace washing over her. With the help of George and Bill and with Khan providing his unique insight, there was nothing she couldn't overcome.

"Let the adventure begin," Jessie whispered to herself, feeling the feline warmth on her lap and the unwavering support of her friends. Together, they would face the unknown and emerge victorious.

THE END

Acknowledgements

A HUGE THANK YOU to Jane Roberts, of England and Michele K, of Georgia, USA, for their invaluable input as alpha and beta readers of this prequel. Heartfelt thanks are also owed to my Cozy Review team They did a sterling job and made life much easier for me and my editor. As usual, I also thank my editor and my book cover designer, the lovely and talented Eeva who is the Book Khaleesi.

No matter how good my editor and beta readers are, mistakes can still be found in many books even those traditionally published. A thousand pair of eyes is better then a handful If you find any problems with typos, grammar etc, blame the author not the editor, Jane or Michele, and let me know by emailing kj@kjcornwall.com. I strive for perfection but alas, I am human.

About the Author

KJ Cornwall is the pen name of Stephen Bentley, a former British police Detective Sergeant, pioneering Operation Julie undercover detective, and barrister. He now writes in the true crime and crime fiction genres and contributes occasionally to Huffington Post UK on undercover policing, and mental health issues.

He is possibly best known for his bestselling Operation Julie memoir and as co-author of Operation George: A Gripping True Crime Story of an Audacious Undercover Sting.

His Operation Julie book has been optioned and is in development as an 8-part TV series in addition to that huge and unique police operation being pitched to broadcasters as a documentary. He is pleased that *Operation George* has also been optioned for the TV screen.

Stephen is a member of the UK's Society of Authors and the Crime Writers' Association.

With Dominic Smith, Stephen is a part of a writing team in the Undercover Legends series under the pen name of David Le Courageux.

Now a multi-genre author, Stephen also writes cozy mysteries in the pen name of KJ Cornwall.

You can listen to Stephen talking about his Operation Julie undercover days on the BBC Radio 4 Life Changing programme/podcast available 24/7 worldwide on BBC Sounds. And on the same platform, he also contributes to Acid Dream: The Great LSD Plot.

Sign up to the mailing list for news of books by Stephen and KJ Cornwall here[1].

---

1. Newsletterhttps://stephenbentley.eo.page/rz1db

Also By

<u>The publisher asks that you consider leaving a review of this book at the platform where you bought it. They do help!</u>

You can find all books written by Stephen Bentley and his pen names including KJ Cornwall using the Booklinker images below or viewing here.

You can also buy his books direct here.

KJ Cornwall Books2Read page is here. Stephen Bentley Books2Read page is here.

Visit the links by using the QR codes below for more details:

Jessie Harper Cozy Mystery Series

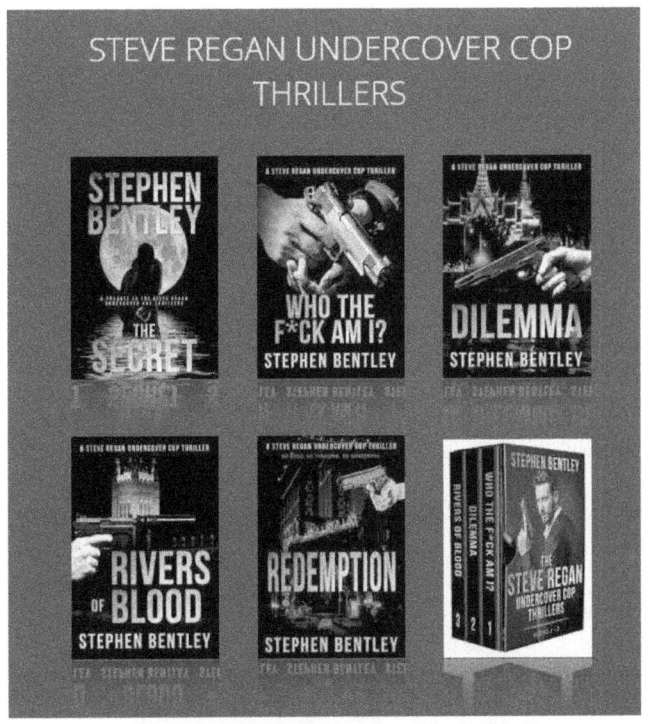

The Steve Regan Undercover Cop Thrillers

The Detective Matt Deal Thrillers

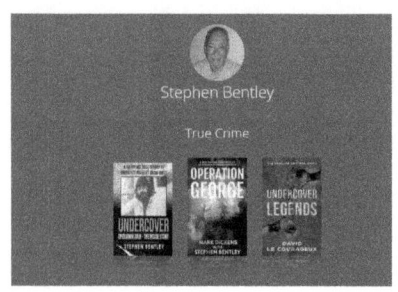

Bestselling True Crime

If you prefer to use QR codes you can find out more about all books written by KJ Cornwall and sign up for the mailing list by scanning the QR code below.

Similarly, you can find full details of true crime books and hard boiled thrillers written by Stephen Bentley by scanning the QR code below.

www.ingramcontent.com/pod-product-compliance
Ingram Content Group UK Ltd.
Pitfield, Milton Keynes, MK11 3LW, UK
UKHW042151171224
452513UK00001B/28